To Ruth &

Best Wishes

Love

Jane Hardoon

GRENADES IN HER UNDERWEAR

and other stories

Anne Hardoon

MINERVA PRESS
LONDON
MONTREUX   WASHINGTON   SYDNEY

First Published 1997 by
MINERVA PRESS
195 Knightsbridge,
LONDON SW7 1RE

2nd Impression 1998

Printed in Great Britain for Minerva Press

GRENADES
IN HER
UNDERWEAR
and other stories

About the Author

Born and educated in South Africa, Anne Levinsky Hardoon has travelled widely. She has lived in London, Tel Aviv and Eilat where she now resides with her family.

Author's Note

Most Israelis have a story... whether it be of the old country, of the grandparents, of escape from pogroms, of surviving the hell of the Holocaust... but the thread that runs through them all is the longing to be in their own country, free of persecution and anti-Semitism. We have all been brought together from the four corners of the world, with different languages, different customs and folklore, likes and dislikes. Call it a melting pot if you will.

Grenades in her Underwear and Other Stories developed as a result of numerous tales of courage and heroism in the face of despair and danger. Although based on many true stories I have made sure that the characters are fictitious and the events cannot pinpoint any one individual. Apart from historical facts most of the events, especially in Israel in itself, are a figment of my imagination. The background of each story however is based on much careful research conducted over many months.

There were so many wonderful people who told me their stories, some amidst tears, others with longing for those left behind. I pay tribute to these people who privileged me by sharing their stories.

Acknowledgements

To all at Minerva Press in appreciation of your hard work
Thanks to Benny Gamlieli for cover photos

And it shall come to pass in that day,

That the Lord will set His hand again a second time

To recover the remnant of his people,

That shall remain from Assyria, and from Egypt,

And from Pathros, and from Cush, and from Elam,

And from Shinar, and from Hamath, and from the islands of the sea,

And he will set up an ensign for the nations,

And will assemble the dispersed of Israel,

And gather together the scattered of Judah

From the four corners of the earth.

Isaiah 11. 11-12

For David Roi with much love

Contents

Grenades in her Underwear

At the turn of the century, *Aliman Alsayida*, or the happy Yemen as the locals called it, was still isolated. In the Jewish quarters of the towns and villages life continued in much the same vein. The young boys were taught to read the holy books and the girls were prepared for an early betrothal by learning to cook, weave, embroider and care for the family. Young Sayida and her cousin Rochel had both been betrothed and accompanied with much fanfare to the neighbouring town where they were taken into their respective husbands' family homes. Both had been miserable and homesick and so, without much ado, had set out at dawn one morning on the long, arduous journey back to their childhood homes.

"Rochel I'm so tired... could we rest awhile?" Dark eyes rimmed with black kohl gazed up at her cousin pleadingly.

The older girl looked around nervously and nodded. "The way is longer than I thought, and we must get home before dark. Yes we will rest here..."

She pointed to the boulders, but Sayida scuffed the burning sand with her heel, searching for the cooler layer underneath. She sank down gratefully lifted her skirt above her leggings and removed her worn-out dust-covered sandals. She dug her feet into the ochre desert sand, watching the grains trickle through her toes. Rochel removed the black hood, wiped her wet forehead with her sleeve and then replaced the head-dress.

"Do you think they'll come looking for us and take us back to the village?" Sayida looked at her cousin in trepidation. "Oh Rochel I couldn't bear it. I want to be with my family, not with his family."

"Just as I don't want to be with Shalom and his family..."

"They were good to me... Chaim didn't touch me, but he looked at me so strangely some days that I was fearful... Why did we have to be married? Rochel we're too young... aren't we too young? Say we're too young," she demanded of her companion.

The older girl, no more than ten years old, nodded wordlessly and for some minutes neither girl said anything. Sayida thought longingly of her mother. Would she be glad to see her, or would she be angry that she'd run away from her husband's family. She remembered how she'd cried all the way to the next town, the black kohl running rivulets down her young cheeks. Had it only been a few weeks? It seemed months since she'd felt her mother's arms around her, hugging her in farewell, her whispered assurances, the spicy *hilbeh* odour emanating from her warm body... She dusted her feet and hurriedly put on her sandals.

"Come on Rochel, I'm ready... hurry, hurry please. I want to see my mother, and I want to eat *lakhookh*," she said, thinking of the pancakes, made from dura flour.

The girls had left just before daybreak and in their haste hadn't thought to take water or pita bread with them. They had crept out of their in-laws' homes breathlessly, anxious not to wake any of the sleeping occupants, and hand in hand they had set out into the desert.

"Are we going in the right direction?" Sayida asked.

"Yes... Look at that bush, the one over there," Rochel pointed. "I piled those stones one on top of the other... on the way here... when we stopped to eat."

The sun had slowly made its fiery way across a cloudless sky and, now on high, mercilessly beat down on the cracked parched earth, playing games with them. The shimmer of water ahead, no water... only more sand and more sand. They squinted into the bright light as they trudged on. A movement ahead, no more than a ripple, as the grains of sand fell inwards, brought them to an abrupt halt. The hot sand heaved and slithered forward, almost camouflaging the viper.

"An evil eye... evil eye... following us." Rochel's hands were wet with perspiration, and she trembled.

"No... a poisonous snake," Sayida said matter-of-factly, watching the slithering track of heaving sand as it slowly disappeared.

"Aren't you thirsty, Rochel? Why didn't we bring water?" Sayida tried wetting her lips with saliva, but her mouth was dry and her throat burned. "How much further?"

"By nightfall we'll be home... don't worry." Rochel didn't sound very convincing though. She'd been having her doubts. The last time they'd taken this route they had travelled on donkeyback and had been accompanied by their fathers and brothers. Now they were alone... oh so alone. "Sayida... perhaps we shouldn't have come..."

"But you said that we were closer to our town than the one we came from. We can't go back now," the younger girl said petulantly.

They were silent for some time as they made their way along a track, winding up the steep mountainside, and then carefully picked their way down rock-strewn terrain until they were able to walk in the valley between two towering rock formations, passing sparse bushes and an occasional tree. The parched earth powdered under their feet. Sayida stopped abruptly. Her bony fingers dug into her cousin's flesh.

"Look..." she whispered as she pointed a shaking finger at the black speck in the distance. It grew slowly larger, while the two gazed hypnotised with fear.

"It's an evil spirit... I know it," cried the younger girl trembling. It took on shape and outline, until they could make out a man astride a donkey. The beast of burden carried a *koffiya* turbaned man who frowned, his black eyes wrinkling in puzzlement as he surveyed the two young girls.

Rochel tensed. "Let's run Sayida. He will kill us."

"No, no, he will help us. He is one of ours. Come we will talk to him."

They stood stock-still as the man rode towards them. The glint of a dagger caught their eyes and Sayida grasped her cousin's hand tightly. He's a Moslem," she whispered hoarsely, her face paling.

He greeted them in surprise. "What are two young girls doing alone in the desert, far from any village or township?"

"We ran on ahead," the younger girl said quickly, hoping he would believe them. "The men are following behind."

"Yes, yes following behind," added Rochel relieved at her cousin's presence of mind. They watched fearfully as the stranger put his hand under his robe and withdrew the flat pita bread.

"Would you like to eat?"

They nodded and took the bread hesitantly. Neither girl dared break a piece although they looked at it longingly.

"Here take another pita..." said the donkey rider, watching them. They said nothing and he was silent for a moment, then he turned the donkey in the direction he'd come. "Please return to the men," he ordered. "It is dangerous for two young girls to be alone on the road." He waved in farewell.

"Thank... you..." Sayida managed throatily, remembering her manners. They waited until he'd disappeared from view, before they moved on.

"If we don't get back by nightfall, we may see ghosts." Rochel looked over her shoulder nervously.

Sayida stood stock-still, her pulse hammering in her temples. "Which ghosts do you mean?" she asked quaveringly, and looked quickly behind, then to the left and to the right. She stiffened. "I see... I see a ghost!"

"Where?" Rochel squinted in the direction of the trembling finger. "No, that's water... come, we can drink at last."

The water moved away from them and no matter how much they hurried towards it, the shimmer stayed the same distance from them. Discouraged, they stopped to rest again.

"I don't know of any good ghosts, only those who put the evil eye on you," ventured Sayida, hoarsely. Her lips were cracked and dry.

"Water... If only we had water... I'm so thirsty," Rochel gasped. "Why didn't you ask the Moslem for water?" She stared angrily at Sayida.

"That would have made him suspicious... You forget we said the men were following, and surely they would have carried water." They trudged silently on. When their shadows lengthened and the sky turned yellow and then orange and the earth ahead darkened forbiddingly, they stumbled wearily onto a stony slope, leaving the powdery earth of the desert behind.

They traversed the slope, and climbed another stony hill which gradually descended into terraces dotted with sparse trees and brush.

"Look Rochel..." cried Sayida joyfully.

They gazed down at the town of brown adobe buildings with their whitewashed windows. Behind the town the rugged majesty of the towering granite mountain reached up to the darkening sky like some sleepy giant stretching his limbs. Small pockets of yellow and green cultivated fields spread out like a patchwork quilt, thrown down by the awakening giant.

It was dark when they finally reached the Jewish Quarter. Children playing in the narrow lanes noticed them and called...

"Rochel and Sayida... where have you been?"

"Sayida, Sayida..."

She was in her mother's arms and she laughed in joy. Safe at last. It was so good to be back home, and she breathed in the familiar spicy odour. She withdrew the pita bread from under her armpit. It was soggy with perspiration but her mother took it gratefully. "Come my daughter, you will wash and we will eat together. Then we will discuss your future. We must not forget that you are wed and we shall have to inform the family that you are safe with us, but you cannot stay." Her black kohl-lined eyes shone with a mixture of joy and sadness.

"Uma, I cannot go back," Sayida cried in anguish. "I want to stay with you and with Abbeh."

"We will see... you are an *alkhanaka*... a runaway bride... so your father will decide," her mother said briefly.

The dawn brought its sounds and smells. Thick spiced coffee brewing, the smell of newly baked pita on the clay taboon, the crowing of roosters and the chirping of birds mixed with the call of the muezzin from the mosque nearby, and the chanting in the Quarter, of the men, their phyllacteries strapped around the arm in prayer. Sayida was unaware of these sounds, for she'd slept soundly. Her mother woke her gently.

"Come little one, we must go to the well for water... You will help me today with the chores and we will talk."

She handed the already dressed Sayida a clay jar and together they made their way to the well. They walked together, mother and daughter. Each had black braided hair covered with the black hoods bordered with decorative gold thread. Many of the women were already there and they gossiped of the events of the previous day. Some of the young women broke into song and their clear, throatily nasal voices carried with the wind back to the Quarter, where the men and young boys paused in the midst of the ancient Hebrew script, lifted their eyes from the books, listened, and then hurriedly resumed their chanting.

The jars were heavy and water slopped out as Mother placed one of them on Sayida's head. "Careful my daughter..." she said as she lifted the second jar onto her shoulder, "if you spill the water, we will be left without the means to cook the grains and the soup."

The Jewish Quarter was at its busiest. The sounds of hammering mingled with the prayers. People went about their business, men taking grains, *samneh* and dates to the suk to exchange them for chillis, cloth and chicken. Women swept the floors, pounded the dura into flour, baked bread, weaved, embroidered and gossiped.

"May I go now to help Abbeh?" asked Sayida eagerly.

"Yes, go and help your father..." said her mother smiling.

The girl ran off excitedly. Father had wept in his happiness at seeing her last evening but had been angry too that she and Rochel had endangered themselves needlessly. After much discussion, he had agreed that she should stay at home until she was a little older when she would join her husband Chaim and his family. They would send word to the next town. Sayida knew that she must one day go back to her husband for was it not said that a woman without a husband is like a bucket without a rope?

Sayida paused at the entrance to one of the clay two-storey houses and watched her uncle trimming the beard of a friend. He had come from Tzada with his tales of the eleven domes, one for every Imam buried in the mosque. An old man sat against the wall smoking the nargillah, and yet another chewed a green leaf, the *Gat*. It made one feel drowsy and good, but she knew that her father disapproved and that none of her family used the weed. A Moslem made his way down the lane and the men of the Quarter stood aside to let him through. From the opposite lane a bearded Jew rode side-saddle on his donkey. When he saw the Moslem he alighted hurriedly, standing aside to let him pass, his eyes averted.

A fly-ridden cow, its ribs sticking out at angles, passed, led by a young Moslem boy. The dung that fell from the cow would be allowed to dry and would be used for the fires.

A man on a makeshift ladder of tree trunks greeted Sayida and she paused, as he smoothed his brush back and forth splashing specks of white paint down the side of the house. What fun, she thought, to be the whitewasher of the arched windows of the Jewish Quarter. She brought her thin brown arms together in make-believe, and then round and out until they came together again, finishing the outline of the windows.

Sayida continued down the lane. The blue-painted scratched and stained doors to the shops, open against the walls, contrasted with the dark entrances. Sacks of grains and dried chillis spilled onto the dried mud floors. She brushed the buzzing flies away impatiently. She was happy. Much as she liked the togetherness of the chores with Uma, she loved above all working the bellows to stoke the fire for her silversmith father.

"Abbeh, I'm here... oh you started without me." She was downcast. "I had to help Uma with the water."

Her father nodded, his black side-curls bobbing up and down. In his mouth he held a long thin pipe, the end of which had been in the burning flames. He worked with delicate precision on a fine piece of silver jewellery. Against the wall squatted her twelve-year-old brother Zecharia, studying Torah. He read aloud and every now and again the father would stop him, to discuss the ambiguity of a particular paragraph.

The girl settled herself down next to her father, never taking her eyes off him. She was fascinated by his artistry and wished she too could learn, but this was a skill passed from father to son, and before Zecharia there was Ben David and before Ben David, Moshe. The latter, however, didn't seem to have much interest in jewellery, and together with his uncle and cousin concentrated on making silver and gold hilts for swords and daggers, although the Jews themselves were not allowed to carry them.

Father looked up and nodded at his daughter. She rose to work the bellows. The sparks flew and the new wood began to burn slowly. Soon there was a roaring fire again and Sayida smiled happily.

A shadow appeared at the doorway and Father looked up. He rose to greet the newcomer and they spoke rapidly. Father withdrew some rhials from a tin in the corner and paid the stranger.

"Abbeh?" Zecharia looked at him questioningly when the stranger had departed.

"The *Akel*... the Imam is again collecting taxes... Read." Father nodded at the open book, and saying no more replaced the blowpipe between his lips and resumed working. The boy took up the book and began to read in a sing-song voice. Father listened and withdrew his pipe once to correct the boy and explain the passage.

Sayida listened intently. She loved the ancient language and wished she too could learn to read but again it was the boys only who were taught. She sighed. Even the youngest, little Avraham, his nose oozing yellow snot, had begun to learn the alphabet. Only she and her little sister Hodiah weren't being taught. She had heard it said that there was one young girl and one alone, who'd learned to read.

Sayida resolved to learn one day, but she kept the resolve to herself. "Abbeh..." she began hesitantly. "Are we selling jewellery today?"

Father blinked his eyes rapidly in acknowledgement, but it was only when he'd completed the intricate filigree that he removed the blowpipe. "Yes my daughter, we will go to the Moslem family who have ordered these silver rings and bracelets. Their son is to be married soon."

Sayida clapped her hands excitedly. She enjoyed going with him to sell to the Moslems. It was a chance to go out beyond the confines of the Jewish Quarter. The Moslem women were always kind to her and offered her fruit. Zecharia closed his book and, rising, he dusted himself down. He too liked these brief trips into a different world.

Father wrapped the silver pieces in a cloth, tying it securely. They made their way through the busy lanes, nodding here, greeting there and now and again Father stopped to chat with a friend. Sayida and her brother always felt important on these trips. They knew that some of their friends envied them these excursions and would be waiting to hear whether anything exciting had happened.

The hustle and bustle was greater outside than it was in the Jewish Quarter. Men sat in teahouses and chatted or smoked their waterpipes. Others crowded around the piles of *Gat* buying the leaves for the afternoon and evening get-togethers, where the *koffiya* turbaned men would chew, consuming great amounts of water. Women, their black veils covering their faces from the outside world of strange men, shopped for fruit, vegetables, chillies and cloth. Sayida never failed to marvel at the huge piles of garlic, chillies and spices. She loved the smell of the spices and the noise of the vendors. They passed an old man, his arms raised, palms up, a wooden walking stick swinging from his elbow. Men squatted on the ground, their upturned, black-bearded faces engrossed in what he was saying. "Abbeh what is happening over there?" asked young Zecharia, interested.

"He is talking about Allah and his greatness," Father answered briefly, hurrying them along.

A scribe, his bearded face frowning in concentration, sat on a wooden packing case penning a contract or a letter for his client who, bending towards him, explained what it was he wanted written.

There was a sudden commotion ahead. A couple of Moslems had turned on an unfortunate Jew, beating him, pulling his side-curls while he, bending away from them in fear tried to protect his face with his forearms. A blob of saliva landed squarely on his head. As suddenly as it had started, the commotion ended and the Jew disappeared down the alley way.

Sayida and Zecharia were shocked. "Come my children," said Father urging them on past the stalls. He himself often sold jewellery where some of the other Jews had taken up ground space at the far end of the suk.

"Abbeh, what happened? Why did the Moslems attack the Jew? and who is he?" Zecharia asked with a mixture of fear and sadness.

"I can only guess," answered Father, his eyes darting left and right, wary of anything untoward. "Perhaps they didn't like the prices, or maybe he touched one of the Moslem garbs by mistake... It happens and we must be very careful outside our own quarter. I am sorry you both had to witness it."

They came to the high, clay-brick building and were ushered into the *hajera*, the patio, to wait. Father uncovered his wares and before long the woman of the house entered, greeting them courteously. Her face, plump and shiny, was free of the compulsory veil. It was only amongst the Jews that the Moslem women were allowed to remove their veils. Having made her purchases, the woman turned to the children bidding them help themselves to the fruit she had brought with her.

The muezzin sounded loud and clear as they were leaving and the men in the suk abandoned their wares and hurried off to noon prayers at the mosque.

Time passed slowly in this small community. It had its ups and downs, its births, its deaths. At every festive occasion and especially at Passover, the men prayed and called, "Next year in Jerusalem," as did every Jew in the diaspora.

It was the time of the drought and the crops withered and died. The earth was cracked and parched. The Sabbath meal was now very frugal and Mother foraged for precious vegetables to make soups. Often they went to sleep hungry. Mother thought it wise that Sayida return to her husband, but she begged to remain with them. She knew that one day she would have to be with him, but surely not before she became a woman... with the bleeding. Yes, Rochel had told her, but she hadn't believed her until she'd seen Ben David's wife washing out her bloodstained rags. She knew then that it was true, but if only

Rochel had continued to instruct her. Why did a woman bleed and what connection did it have to making babies? Well she'd just have to ask cousin Rochel again. Maybe she didn't know either.

*

It was many years later in Sharai'im in Rehovot that Sayida had time to think back on those last few months in the Jewish Quarter, when her father and some of the men had met with the stranger from Palestine. There had been fire in his eyes, this Shmuel Yavnieli from over the seas. There was much activity and consultation in the weeks following and when Father was given permission to leave, he had had to train a Moslem to take over his skills. He'd spent many weeks teaching the intricacies of the filigree work, but although his pupil learned quickly, he hadn't the delicacy of Father. When the day of their departure had arrived, they had packed a few meagre belongings and had slipped away as discreetly as possible after taking tearful farewells of the friends and relatives remaining.

Sayida sighed when she thought of those difficult weeks when they'd had to walk most of the way to the sea. Their shoes wore thin and finally were discarded, and they walked on hot stones and sand until their feet were callused and bleeding. They fell ill but there was no medicine other than what Mother and some of the other women prepared from the plants they encountered *en route*. Food was scarce and very hard to come by. Young children, the old and the sick rode on donkeys but Sayida had walked. Many children and old people died along the way... When they finally reached the sea near Aden, it was as though they had arrived in the Promised Land... but no, they had still been so far away from their dream, a whole, swirling, rolling, terrifying, sick-making sea away.

Sayida moved away from the window where she had been watching her granddaughters at play. They had drawn two circles on the ground with a stick and were hopping around, balanced on one leg, kicking a stone. She smiled at their laughter. Her bony face and fiery eyes belied her age, only her wrinkled leathery neck established the years and the hardships. 'It is time to go. I must be very careful, the soldiers are searching this area again,' she mused.

She bent down and pulled an orange crate from under the iron bed. She methodically removed the layers of clothing until she came to a cardboard box. This she opened carefully and withdrew very slowly a couple of pear-shaped indented metal balls. 'The best place for these are my pants...' she chortled. 'Who would think of searching an old woman...'

'Grenades in her underwear?' the Mandate officer would shout. 'The woman is mad.' No one would ever suspect her of doing such things... though she'd been at it for years... ever since she'd joined the underground freedom fighters, the Lehi. Even Chaim her husband didn't know it all. Better he should never know. He had enough to contend with, being the *Mukhtar* of Sharai'im, and having to deal with the problems of the residents and the British soldiers who were forever searching their homes. It took all his energy keeping the people out of trouble. It was to Chaim they came with their problems. It was Chaim this and Chaim that, and it was always he who solved them.

Having filled a woven shopping basket with pita, vegetables, *skhoog* and fruit, she closed the door quietly and ran down the worn stairs. 'I must be careful,' she thought. 'It would be bad if I were to slip.' She remembered suddenly the nail parings she'd put carefully aside. They must be destroyed... or the evil eye... She returned to the room, and carefully collected them one by one. Nothing must be left behind. Her daughter Yehudit met her on the stairs.

"I'll be back later," she said in answer to the unspoken question. She opened the gate and stepped out onto the road.

"*Savta, Savta* Sayida... come play with us," called little Tami breathlessly.

Her heart warmed to this wildfire granddaughter of hers. 'She is so much like I was... only she should have an easier life...' she mused. "No Tami... Yael... I am busy today..."

"*Savta*, can I come with you?" asked Tami, the younger of the two girls, having now lost interest in her game.

"No... not today... some other time." She glanced hurriedly down the road but there were no soldiers about. One couldn't be sure though.

"Please *Savta*, please take me with you," the child begged, following her.

"No... Here take this," she said opening her clenched fist. "Throw these into Garawanie's bonfire... otherwise..."

"Yes *Savta*," said the child meekly. She looked up to see her mother watching her through the open window, and waved. Yehudit leaned out, about to say something, but she thought better of it. The soldiers were everywhere and it was best not to attract attention. She didn't know for sure but she suspected that her mother was involved in the underground. She worried incessantly about her, but knowing how obstinate the old woman was, she kept her peace. She stiffened suddenly. From her vantage point she could see the danger but was unable to do anything about it. She was frozen with fear.

Sayida walked swiftly towards the main road. 'I will take a taxi... the first one I see...' As she neared the corner, her heart missed a beat. Two khaki-clad soldiers were approaching from the other end.

'A taxi... a taxi. Come on taxi...' she begged silently. They were coming nearer when she spied the battered cab as it turned the corner. She flagged it frantically and it came to a stop with a screech of brakes. The soldiers were now about twenty metres away when she felt the tugging of her skirt.

"*Savta*... I'm here." Her granddaughter looked up at her appealingly.

"Quickly get in..." she ordered the child urgently, as she pushed her into the back seat. "Here sit on my knees and don't lean backwards." The soldiers bent to peer in at the occupants... an old woman with a child on her knees seemed harmless enough, and they waved the cab on.

As the car gathered speed, Sayida breathed easier. 'What did Abbeh always tell us? Something about the heart... Ah yes, when the heart is anxious, troubles are spurred. I must at all costs remain calm. What luck the child followed me after all. Without Tami on my knees they may well have searched me.' "Tami what did you do with the nail parings?"

"Yael took them to throw in Garawanie's bonfire. I'm afraid of Garawanie... he's a witch."

The cab driver turned to look at them. "Could it be Sayida? It is many years since I saw you... but I would know you anywhere."

Sayida was startled. She searched her memory. Why yes, surely this man had taught her to read and write, so many years ago. How he had changed.

"Shimon of course... you are no longer a teacher?"

He chuckled. "I do both... I drive during the day and at night I teach, but I never again had a student like you. How goes it with you?"

They chatted for a while and then were silent. Sayida visualised those faraway years, when in two creaking wooden boats they'd set sail from Aden. Choppy seas, most of the occupants seasick, huddling together in fear with very little room to move, Abbeh struck with fever and not a drop of water left on the boat. They had signalled the second boat and with much manoeuvring and difficulty they had come as close as possible, so that they could hear Moshe as he shouted into the wind through his cupped hands. Yes they still had some of the precious liquid but the problem was how to get it to Abbeh. She remembered the plank with which they'd bridged the two boats... someone fast and small... she'd volunteered fearfully... for her beloved father she'd overcome her terror and had crossed the dark blue rolling sea with its white flecks and spray. The men had cheered her when, her heart pumping quickly, she'd made it back without mishap.

"Thank you my daughter," Abbeh had managed to gasp and she'd seen Uma's eyes glowing with pride. She remembered every detail vividly and so she should, having related the story to her own children time and time again.

They turned into a rough bumpy track and the cab came to a stop. Sayida alighted and with a "Wait for me" to Tami and the driver, she made her way towards a small house partly hidden in the trees. She handed over the grenades and the food which she'd brought for the underground and which would immediately be taken to the safe house in a different area, and hurried back to the car.

"My relatives... I brought them food," she explained, although her teacher hadn't asked.

"You had just married when you came to learn with me and you now have grandchildren," chuckled Shimon watching Sayida through the rear-view mirror.

"No, Chaim and I were betrothed in Yemen when I was a child, but it was only after he and his family arrived a few years after we did, that we lived together as man and wife." Sayida thought fondly of her husband. Chaim was a good man, a loving husband and father. Those first years had been so difficult. How happy they had been to arrive in their own land. The men had walked to Jerusalem and realised their lifelong dream.

They had been settled near the orange groves in Rehovot and Sayida grimaced when she recalled how they'd had to live in a cowshed, sharing cramped quarters with a few scrawny cows. The summers had been hell and they were covered in mosquito bites. The winters had been worse when the rains had turned the surroundings into a quagmire, and they had been perpetually cold with chapped lips and chilblained hands.

The hostility of the inhabitants, especially of the Ashkenazi pioneers, had bewildered them at first but they had accepted it stoically and with patience borne of years of suffering and degradation. Sayida had joined her family picking oranges in the groves for which they were paid a pittance. The hours were long and backbreaking and the men, Father, Ben David and Moshe amongst them, had found jobs as night watchmen, and they had managed on very little sleep, coming straight from one job to the next at dawn. Shimon broke the silence again.

"Whose child is this little Tami?"

"The second child of my daughter Yehudit and her husband Zecharia."

"You had a brother Zecharia, didn't you?"

"Yes, he lives now in Canada. Before you get to Rehovot turn left at the railway tracks. I will direct you," said Sayida. She'd promised an Arab woman to intercede on her behalf. The husband had taken another wife and had driven his first out of the house by saying three times "I divorce you." This first wife was living in a hovel near Sharai'im and working the groves. She'd been forbidden to see her son Abdullah. "I'll do what I can," Sayida had promised her.

The olive trees grew here in abundance and Sayida with the child in tow made her way to the house of Abu Abdullah. They were welcomed with expansive Moslem hospitality. The second wife brought in fruit, sardines, pita and coffee and then withdrew silently.

"Please eat," Abu Abdullah asked graciously of Sayida and the child. Sayida spoke of the weather, of the harvest, of the groves. She asked after Abdullah but still she didn't eat.

"*Siyit* Sayida, I will be insulted if you do not eat," insisted the errant husband.

She sat up and said quietly. "I have eaten here before and it was the mother of Abdullah who served me. I will eat only if she is here."

The Arab groaned, his head in his hands and reflected for a while. "Abdullah," he called.

"Yes Father?" the boy answered respectfully, entering the room.

"Call your mother... She must come immediately, so that our guest will eat."

Before long the boy returned with his bashful mother. The husband beckoned to her to come forward. "Our honoured guest will eat only if you will serve."

Sayida nodded, accepting the fruit from her friend. "Abdullah's mother must stay here, with him. A boy needs his mother."

"Ahhhhh," said Abu Abdullah nodding to himself. "Yes I will take her back. You are right *Siyit* Sayida. You are a wise woman."

The street was in an uproar when they returned. The soldiers were everywhere. Sayida quickened her pace. If they were to search her room who knew what they might find. She sent her grandchild to play and crossed the road. She found Chaim in earnest conversation with one of the soldiers.

"If you return the gun we will not search the house, I promise. I'll shake your hand on that," said the tall uniformed man looking intently at Chaim. "In fact we'll stop all the searches down this street."

Chaim, his beard grizzled and flecks of grey streaking his thick black hair turned to his wife. "Sayida, the children are hiding in fear. We must have quiet in the area. Do we have the gun?" he asked in Yemenite Arabic.

Sayida spoke quietly and Chaim asked the soldier to wait. He returned with the weapon handing it to the soldier who shook his hand and left.

The neighbours crowded around Chaim. "Do you think they will punish us for taking a gun?" asked one.

"Perhaps they will make renewed searches?" asked another. They were all anxious. The soldiers were often brutal and the searches were humiliating.

"No," Chaim shook his head. "The soldier gave his hand that there would be no more searches here, and you all know that with the English the handshake is a gentleman's honour."

*

It was cold and the two figures huddling in the dark shivered. The street emptied of people and they waited a while longer. A woman emerged from a doorway. She looked left then right and crossed the road. She carried a woven basket held close to her. As she neared the shadows, she bent down as though to adjust her shoes and she hummed softly to herself.

"Here Shosh... we're here."

She straightened and melted into the shadows. Sayida smiled, relieved. "I thought I'd never make it. The streets have been so busy tonight. Here take this and give me your bag." They exchanged bags and she departed. "May God be with you."

"You too Shosh..." they said in unison, using her code name.

The men waited until she had disappeared from view and then hurriedly emerged from the shadows and began pasting the posters on walls and doorways.

Sayida never missed the Monday and Thursday broadcasts... "You are listening to the Voice of the Hebrew Underground, this is the radio station of the Freedom fighters of Israel," she recognised that deep young voice, "the voice of those fighting for the liberation of the Jewish people and its historic homeland."

The fedayeen raids continued, the British curfews and searches continued... desperate immigrants, refugees of the Holocaust began arriving only to be turned away by the Mandate soldiers.

Sayida felt drained. She worked day and night... she made do with very few hours of sleep. The night shadows hid her comings and goings... guns, grenades, dynamite, posters, and pamphlets called the *Hekhazit* (the Front), for the young Lehi fighters, passed through her hands. She attended secret meetings, brought food for the men who'd escaped from the prison in Latrun, cared for Chaim, the children and grandchildren. She hadn't a moment to herself. When had she ever, come to think of it. She'd delivered her own babies with no outside help, cut and knotted their umbilical cords herself, washed and swaddled them and brought them up to be law-abiding citizens. Her black piercing eyes glowed with pride when she thought of them, those same eyes which turned fierce and cold when faced by the enemy.

She remembered the desperate cries of the refugees turned away from the shores, and her eyes narrowed. The Haganah had joined forces with the underground and gunfire had blazed from Acre to Gaza and from Jerusalem to the sea. They blew up radar stations and sank three British patrol boats. There were floggings, arrests, hangings and deportations to Eritrea, where some two hundred and fifty-one prisoners, including Lehi members, among them friends of Sayida, had been sent, many to be killed out there.

'When will it end?' she mused silently. 'The life we lead is no life at all, wondering when we'll be caught, who will be the next, how many of these oppressors we can put out of action. When will we have our own country without the Mandate authorities at one end and the Arab threat at the other. I'm so tired.'

Winter with its torrential rains came and went. The long, hot summer frayed nerves and tempers. The violence escalated and the cries of the desperate refugees from the blackened hell of Europe, turned away from the shores of Palestine, continued to haunt the Jews in the Yishuv. In the sweltering heat of July a wing of the King David Hotel in Jerusalem, the headquarters of the Mandate Government and military command, was blown up, killing eighty officers and soldiers and wounding many more.

Violence escalated, spilled into the streets, and army bases were attacked. When in the following year the Exodus carrying four thousand five hundred refugees tried to land in Haifa, the British soldiers herded them into three small freighters and transported them to Cyprus. Sayida had been down at the shore having brought weapons to some of her comrades and the wails and screams of desperate men, women and children had brought tears to her eyes and a welling hatred of their oppressors. She knew those sounds would haunt her for the rest of her life.

The Mandate authority was by now at its wits' end, and finally passed the problem of Palestine to the United Nations. The latter sent an investigatory commission which ratified the original British Peel Commission of 1939 that the British Mandate be terminated and that Palestine be partitioned into two; a Jewish state and an Arab state. It was a cold November 29th 1947 when thousands of Palestinian Jews sat glued to their wireless sets listening to the United Nations Assembly vote. With a more than two-thirds majority the Commission voted for the partition recommendation.

The relief was great and a feeling of joy swept through the settlements, people hugged one another and strangers in the streets formed circles and danced. It was bedlam outside. Sayida watched from her window. She felt bereft. The land for the Jews had been whittled away and did not include the heart, Jerusalem, which was to be internationalised. Where were Bethlehem, Nablus? They had risked their lives for this moment and the feeling was bitter-sweet.

She knew too that once the British colonial forces pulled out the Arabs would go to war with them, well they would fight and win, no doubt about it. How much more suffering, how much more bloodshed before the state of Israel could live in peace with her neighbours?

Immigration would now become legal and suddenly her heart soared with relief. Perhaps Rochel and her family would come together with thousands of Jews from Yemen: she hadn't seen cousin Rochel since leaving the Jewish Quarter so many, many years ago. She had heard that when Rochel's parents had died, her young brother Yehiel had been smuggled from house to house, then from village to village until he'd managed to cross the border, and been brought to the Yishuv to join his older brothers who'd made *aliyah* so many years before.

The Imam had proclaimed new laws for the Jews: most were aimed at protecting them, but the one that hurt most was the protection of the authorities over orphans who were rounded up, converted to Islam and kept in orphanages until old enough to be drafted into the army. There was no other way to save these poor orphans other than smuggle them out of Yemen, and many lives were risked and lost in trying to save the children.

Her eyes misted when she thought back on that long and dangerous trek through the parched desert sands she and Rochel had undertaken, and their fear. Would they have undertaken the journey had they known just how dangerous it was? She recalled the Moslem on the donkey. "Why are you girls alone? Do you not know that it is very dangerous for two young girls to be alone in the desert?" 'I've lived through so many dangers since then and the greatest is still to come,' thought Sayida wearily as she turned away from the window.

Arab attacks now intensified and the British began preparations to withdraw. The Jews prepared for the inevitable. War would come, most likely as soon as the State of Israel was proclaimed. Sayida spent longer hours as courier. They now needed more and more weapons and she carried them on her person to the orange groves, sometimes to Yavniel, to Rehovot, to Tirat Shalom, or to the dunes where they changed hands, always undercover, always with whispers.

The cold December sun shone weakly through the dark menacing clouds, only to be covered by a swiftly moving black cloud. Sayida shivered under her frayed jacket. At dawn she had awoken with a foreboding of things to come. As usual she had prepared breakfast for the family. The house was cold and her fingers found difficulty in prising open the floor tile, under which she kept the hand grenades. 'Today I'll take only two grenades and the rest tonight. It can't be helped...'

She hurried out of the house and at the end of the road she hailed a cab. She alighted on the main road and made her way through the trees, stopping every now and again to listen. She heard the whistle and as she turned towards the direction it had come from, she heard a rush of footsteps and "Halt who goes there?" She froze on the spot, not daring to move, then as the soldiers came upon her she raised her hands. 'I'm finished,' she thought. 'They will imprison me or as a parting gift before they pull out, send me to Africa.' She looked at them impassively although her heart beat rapidly and she felt that if she opened her mouth she would gasp...

"Search her," ordered the officer of his underling.

Sayida felt the hands on her body and she held her breath. If he frisked her at the sides he would possibly overlook the grenade. "What have you in the basket?" growled the officer irritably, "and what are you doing here in the groves?"

"I work here during the season..." Sayida replied.

"Anything?" asked the officer.

The soldier shook his head in disappointment. "Nothing unless she has something hidden in her underwear."

'Ahhh, the end for me. How will Chaim manage without me, the children, the little ones...' she thought, her face still impassive.

"No, she's an old woman. What do you think she'll carry in her underwear? A grenade?" and the officer guffawed.

"Go ahead, old woman, go to your work."

She watched them turn and leave, her heart still pounding in her ears.

A Divorce of Convenience

The corrugated iron roofs reflected the heat of the midday sun. All was quiet in the dorp of Skoenesville. The children were still in school, but the little ones would be out soon, with the clanging of the bell. The houses were clones, replicas of one another, square, with the front door set in the middle, latticed bay windows on either side and sheltered by a pillared stoep or verandah. Small gardens and backyards differed only in the effort put into them. Some had struggling greenish-yellow lawns dotted with drooping flowers, but most had been neglected and left to shrivel and die.

The second year of the drought had brought water prices up and most of the townspeople couldn't afford the luxury, and of course watering hours were reduced to one hour a day, at sunset only.

Josh Feinglass peered at himself through the dusty broken mirror. An orange thread had obstinately lodged itself in his second molar. "Got you," he said aloud as he flicked the citrus string to the floor. He smoothed his ginger moustache and noticing a pimple at the side of his nose he leaned forward and squeezed, watching with satisfaction as the yellow pus oozed out. 'I really need to exercise more, walk more.' He patted his bulging midriff. 'God I'm only thirty-two going on forty-two,' he thought irritably. 'Why did Uncle Barney have to leave me this shop when he died? I'd still have been living in Kroonstad or probably gone to Wits to study. No, then I wouldn't have met Ettie...' He thought of his excitable wife. She'd been brought up in Skoenesville but had gone to school in Bloemfontein. That's where they had met ten years ago at the party thrown for the visiting Israeli dance troupe. He remembered her attempt at sophistication when she'd accepted a cigarette from one of the dancers. Josh had stood aside watching and when the young Israeli had leaned over to light Ettie's cigarette, something in Josh had stirred and he'd been relieved when Ettie, losing interest in the young fellow had moved off, holding the cigarette precariously between her fingers. He'd sauntered over and introduced himself. How surprised he'd been to hear that she came from the same small community as his Uncle Barney. Ettie had been pretty in a buxom way, her blonde hair swept up in the fashionable chignon of the late fifties. They'd hit it off immediately and had married nine months later.

Josh moved over to the store entrance. Business was very quiet and he leaned against the door frame. 'Must be the drought, the farmers are buying less, and even the labourers are making do with less,' he sighed.

A hot wind seemed to spring up suddenly and he watched as a whirl of dust arose across the scorched veldt, whirled and twirled cone-shaped, and headed across the sparse bushveldt towards the dorp and the General Stores.

He turned hastily and closed the door, viewing the swirling dust-storm from a dirt-smeared window. It died down quickly and Josh stared at the chocolate wrappings, scraps of newspaper and torn paper bags which the wind had brought and which, with an almost uncanny precision, it had deposited at the shop front.

The flies returned with a vengeance and Josh turned irritably. "Johannes man where are you? Get rid of these bleddy flies man."

"Yes'm baas I spray like this..." said the African, grabbing the DDT pump. Sweat glistened on his muscular arms as they moved backwards and forwards. The flies flew lazily up towards the ceiling, seemingly impervious to the poison.

Johannes disappeared out the back way and Josh moodily surveyed his stock. On the left-hand side of the shop he had piles of fabrics, the yellows, reds, blues and greens of the materials livening up the gloomy interior. On the opposite side he and Johannes had arranged the groceries. The latter had shown a penchant for artistry and had arranged the canned goods into pyramids, which every now and then collapsed and rolled every which way, especially when some mischievous child would slyly pull out one of the bottom tins.

The shrill ring of the old black telephone brought him hurrying over to the side room which served as an office, but was used only once a month when Ettie came to do the books. "So what's new, darl?" he asked his wife. "Yes, yes I have some of that pink viyella left, how much do you want? No I don't think I have six yards, at the most four... I'll bring it anyway."

Ettie was sewing frantically, everything from dresses to curtains to sheets and even pillowslips. It was as if she were preparing a trousseau, but not for a marriage – unless you could call making aliyah to Israel a marriage. Yes, why not a marriage to a new country? He listened a while longer without saying anything, although he nodded a couple of times. 'Now what does she have to tell me that's so exciting?' he wondered silently. 'Something she can't tell me on the phone just in case someone's listening?'

He rang up the cash register and handed the customer a loaf of white bread and a bottle of Coca Cola. The man, his dark brown knees showing through his ragged trousers, turned and made his way to the end of the store stoep, where he squatted and brushing aside some dust with a gnarled hand, settled himself down to lunch.

It was late in the afternoon when Ettie swept into the shop like a hurricane. "Hi darl," she called happily. "If Mohammed won't come to the mountain then the mountain will come to Mohammed." She giggled at her cleverness. "I think our lift will be on the way soon." She pulled her skirt to both sides with her hands and twirled.

"Lift, shmift, who's talking about a lift when I can't sell this shop? How do you think we'll live in Israel without money?" he asked plaintively. "Even with the allowed allocation there won't be enough to set up in business let alone buy a new flat. The republic allows only a very limited amount of capital to be taken out the country."

"Wait till you hear Bella's news... she phoned this morning." Ettie looked at him with a slight smile. She'd lost weight and much of her earthiness had disappeared, especially after she'd lost the baby.

"Okey dokes darl, shoot. What did Bella of Johannesburg have to tell you that's so exciting?"

"She called to say that..." She turned to see whether she was being overheard and then continued in hushed tones. "That she and Anthony are divorcing."

"Good God! No!"

She laughed. "Yes, they're divorcing so that each will be able to take out capital, which will come to a lot more than the amount a couple is allowed."

"So?" Josh was puzzled. What had this to do with himself and Ettie?

"So you and I get divorced and..."

"No, absolutely no... I don't want to hear anything more about this." Hurt shone out of Josh's blue eyes and they brimmed suddenly.

Ettie looked at him in surprise. She was fast losing patience with her unimaginative spouse. She pouted. "What's with you, darl? You know it's only temporary, only till we get to Israel and then we'll have a second wedding."

Josh shook his head obstinately.

"You've no spunk. You were so enterprising once. Come on, what are you afraid of?"

Josh was silent, the hurt still apparent in his soulful eyes. "How could you suggest we divorce for some extra hard cash? When we sell the shop we'll manage on the allowed capital and the rest we'll invest and get monthly income."

"You're actually afraid of losing me?" she giggled teasingly.

"I refuse to do anything underhand and yes, I am afraid of losing you."

"Lose me? No way... oh come on Josh, let me go up to Jo'burg and talk to Bella and..."

Nothing remains stagnant forever, such is the way of the world. When the first news of another gold dust find became known the length and breadth of the country, the surrounding towns and villages began to take on a different look. True the red dust remained and the parched earth cracked a little more, but there was a sense of excitement and expectation the likes of which hadn't been felt in these parts in many a year. Skoenesville, from a sleepy yawning farming township in the flatlands of the Orange Free State began to stir with ripples of unrest.

People collected in groups on the streets and on Sunday afternoons on the stoeps, to exchange news and gossip. Unlike the pioneers of the Wild West where men staked their claim to patches of land and then began prospecting, the government sent their own experts, their heavy equipment, their drills, their drivers and their bossboys. As interest grew, strangers drifted into town in their Pontiacs, Plymouths and Hillmans. It was just such a stranger who wandered into Josh's store one day to buy a pack of Lucky Strikes.

He looked around noncommittally, almost uninterested, and said offhandedly. "You the owner of this joint, man?"

Josh nodded absently.

"You maybe interested in selling, man?"

"What is it you need?" asked Josh absently. "Groceries, materials? Here we have some fine..."

"Ach no man, the shop!"

Josh stood stock-still, his mouth agape and the vein in his temple pulsing. "You, you mean...?"

"Yes, man, that's exactly what I mean."

Within days of negotiating, the sale was concluded, and Josh and Ettie were free to plan their impending divorce. She had finally made him see reason. They began sorting their belongings, and when the Venters, who'd coveted the house for some time, finally agreed to the price, they called in the packers.

The divorce was quick and unemotional. It was all happening so fast. It seemed unreal, like watching a play on stage. It wasn't happening to them but to someone else and they were the onlookers. Application for their allowed capital allotment was approved, but when transferred into dollars it somehow seemed to shrink.

It was the beginning of the frost, when nightfall came early and people hurried home to roaring fireplaces, that, after a flurry of farewells in Skoenesville and then again in Johannesburg, the newly divorced couple were airborne and on their way to their new land, destination Tel-Aviv.

Time lost all meaning, and so two years later it was a very different Ettie Feinglass Davidi who entered the portals of the Sharon Hospital. Her right hand grasped an extended belly and she leaned back in her efforts to retain her balance. Her tall, gangling second husband brought up the rear with the anxious excitement of a new father-to-be.

Shimon had come into Ettie's life when Josh, frustrated at his inability to learn Hebrew and his hurt at Ettie's reluctance to remarry, had finally taken up his brother's offer of a partnership in Johannesburg, and returned to the Republic.

Shimon Davidi was tall where Josh had been short, thin where Josh had been stocky. As opposed to Josh's thinning hair, Shimon was endowed with a crown of black wiry hair, which continued down his neck and covered his shoulders and chest. He was the complete opposite of Josh and Ettie had been swept off her feet by his rugged good looks. He worked for a taxi company and his ambition was to have his own taxi, although he hadn't the means to invest in the rather expensive licence; that is not until he met Ettie and began questioning her about her origins, her likes and dislikes. A fare from the Ulpan at Ramat Aviv to Dizengoff Street blossomed into romance and it wasn't long before he presented her to his large family in the Hatikva quarter.

The first year had been hard on Ettie. She hardly saw Shimon who now owned his own cab and worked late night shifts, very often sleeping mornings, when she had to be up for work as a dental assistant. Also the extended family good-naturedly pressured her to produce a son and heir. "Why not a girl?" she would laugh. "No the firstborn must be a boy," remonstrated Shimon's sister.

"Well fortunately it's not up to me..."

At eight minutes past midnight, after concentrated effort and a strangled scream Ettie was delivered of a baby girl.

"Is she OK? Ten fingers, ten toes and all that sort of a thing?" she asked happily, trying to catch a glimpse of the baby.

"Yes all there..." answered the midwife absently, and as Ettie closed her eyes she caught a fragment of something the doctor seemed to be saying. "Sutures... the head very small..." then "Hush..."

"My baby's head small?" she laughed opening her eyes. "Why it runs in my husband's family. His aunt Allegria has a small head."

"Relax and try to get some sleep," suggested the nurse kindly.

Shimon's initial reaction at hearing the news was one of disappointment. He had been expecting a boy. He shrugged. 'Never mind, next time,' he thought. 'A *brit mila* we must have... yes, next time,' and he cheered up, flashing his white teeth at everyone. When he saw his baby daughter for the first time, he was taken aback. "She's not a good-looking baby... but then neither was I and look at me today."

"She'll be all right." Ettie too kept her thoughts to herself. 'As soon as she puts on weight and becomes chubby, she'll be adorable, and the head... so she'll be like Allegria, so what,' she told herself.

On being discharged from the maternity ward, Ettie was given an appointment to bring the baby for skull X-rays at the age of a month. "Just routine..." she was told. At three months they again brought the persistently wailing baby for examinations.

"Is there something wrong?" Ettie asked again. "My husband has an aunt..."

"Just routine. All babies are examined..." the doctor replied evasively.

At six months, the worried parents were told to make an appointment with a specialist. The nearest date was two months hence and the baby was eight months old when the doctor broke the news to them.

"Your baby daughter has what is called microcephalis... in other words," he said gently, "the sutures in her skull are closed. They should remain open until the age of two so that there is space for expansion of the brain, but she was born with the sutures closed. There is very little we can do."

"But surely, doctor..." protested Ettie, the tears coursing down her ashen cheeks. "An operation... something, please?"

"I'm so sorry," the doctor said hesitantly. "You should have been told immediately after the birth that the only possible solution is to put the baby in an institution, where she will be cared for..."

"No!" interrupted Shimon, his eyes blazing. "We don't do such things. We don't put our old people in a home and we will not send our child away either. My wife will care for her."

"It will be increasingly difficult," said the doctor dubiously. The child will probably not live beyond the age of two, and... it would be better to start thinking of having another child as soon as possible."

The heartbroken parents were subdued all the way home. Shimon was shattered, his world fallen apart. To think that he should have fathered such a defective child... no, it must be Ettie's fault. These Ashkenasi Jews seem to have many congenital uh, uh... where had he heard it before? Yes he'd heard something on the radio once. That must be the reason, the genes, Ettie's defective genes; he looked at her resentfully.

They couldn't afford to put the baby in an institution, so she'd have to care for the child, and he, well, he was away most of the time, and he'd go stay with his mother in Hatikva when things got too bad.

Ettie continued weeping. She couldn't stop. She knew that they would have to put the baby into an institution, that soon she wouldn't be able to relieve the child of her pain, wouldn't know how to deal with her anguished cries. She knew though that they couldn't afford the care. All her money and Josh's too had gone to buy Shimon's taxi and as a down payment on the heavily mortgaged flat they'd bought in Givataiyim.

"What are we going to do, Shimon?" Ettie barely got the words out.

"Nothing," he said tersely. "Perhaps the doctors are wrong? No, they're right. I wish they'd told us from the start. That way we wouldn't have brought the baby home at all."

Ettie watched his angry profile and he didn't see her hurt surprise. "No we most certainly would not have abandoned her, even had we known," she said firmly and quietly.

The days dragged by. Ettie, unable to have a night's sleep, looked exhausted. She began to neglect herself and although at first she listlessly went about her chores, as the weeks went by, the flat, once so spotless, now left much to be desired. Shimon was angry and blamed her for everything. He began to stay away even during his off hours, but she didn't care any more. She still gave her full attention to the crying baby, but nothing she did seemed to calm the child. 'Josh wouldn't have deserted me in similar circumstances,' she suddenly mused one day. She hadn't thought much about Josh during these last few months. She knew she'd hurt him, hurt him badly. She didn't know why she hadn't wanted to remarry, not that she hadn't wanted to at the beginning, but what with getting settled, learning Hebrew at the Ulpan and so many endless things to see to, there hadn't been time and then later... well later her sudden freedom had made her feel young and desirable again, and when she realised that Josh wasn't happy in their new surroundings and she knew that she could never return to the old life, she'd decided finally not to remarry him, and he'd returned to South Africa very bitter and very hurt.

The anger hadn't lasted and before long Josh was phoning long distance to find out how she was. When she'd married Shimon she hadn't heard from him again until a mutual friend had arrived in Israel with regards from Josh. When the baby was born she'd written him about her joy. "Please be happy for me Josh, and forgive me for what I did to you..."

Josh hadn't replied but had sent some of the most beautiful baby clothes and five hundred dollars. She'd heard that he was doing very well in Johannesburg and she was glad for him.

The anguished cry brought her back to reality and she hurried over to the crib. She lifted the child and cradled her in her arms rocking her to and fro. "Hush little one, everything will be all right..." The baby seemed to be in pain. 'What am I going to do?' she wondered desperately. 'We'll have to put her into an institution. There'll be a stage where I'll be unable to help her and if it means bringing Shimon home again... Oh God we can't afford it.' She kissed the little forehead, her tears mingling with the baby's. She started suddenly. 'Of course, why didn't I think of it before. Josh will help. Oh I'm sure he'll help.'

Within two weeks she had a reply to her letter. "I've always been there for you and always will be there for you. Just let me know what to send and don't have any hesitations. I have done extremely well since leaving Israel and whatever you want you shall have."

It took weeks before they were able to find a place in one of the overcrowded institutions and it was only through the intervention of Ettie's obstetrician that they were finally given the green light. Arrangements were made and the day arrived when Ettie and her baby daughter were to part for good. Shimon had calmed down and had accepted Josh's help, albeit grudgingly. He knew he didn't have any alternative.

The journey there was silent. Neither of them dared speak, Ettie for fear she'd become hysterical and have her husband turn on her in anger. Shimon didn't dare say anything for fear that Ettie would construe it in the wrong way, and then he knew it would be difficult to control his anger. In his ignorance he still blamed her for the tragedy that had befallen them. Ettie's cheeks were wet and she watched the restless child anxiously.

"I'll come and visit you, sweetheart," she whispered.

Shimon came to a stop. He turned to her. "You stay here and I'll take the carrycot. It'll be better like this, believe me."

She nodded wordlessly bending down to kiss the baby and then she dropped her face into her hands, her body wracked with spasms of sobbing.

When Shimon finally returned after what seemed like an eternity, although only an hour had gone by, his face was a mask, his lips set in a grim line. He didn't look at her and his clenched knuckles were white with the force with which he gripped the steering wheel.

Josh was true to his word and the money arrived the first week of every month straight into their account at the bank. Shimon insisted on dealing with this himself. She'd gone once to visit the baby and had come home wretched and torn with guilt. When she'd finally blurted out that she wished that they hadn't let the baby go, he'd lost his cool and bellowed. "I forbid you to go again. It's not good for you and the quicker you forget her the better."

Ettie was aghast. "You forbid me? How can you forbid me? I'm not your child, Shimon."

His hand connected with her cheek and her head jerked back under the impact of the stinging slap. She was shocked. No one had ever raised a hand to her before. Shimon seemed as shocked as she was. "I'm sorry, Ettie. Please forgive me. I've been under such strain for months. Am I forgiven?"

"As long as you never lay a hand on me again," she retorted icily. Her life seemed to be slowly coming apart at the seams. 'Must be my punishment for what I did to Josh. Oh God why was I so stupid. I had something good going for me and I selfishly threw it away. No, stop thinking such things,' she told herself sternly, but it was no use. Her thoughts turned more and more to her first husband.

Ettie returned to work as a dental assistant, but she and Shimon remained distant with one another. She went to visit the baby again, without telling Shimon, and was informed that the child was now blind and that it would be better if she didn't come in future.

When she mentioned the blindness to her husband, she was once more rewarded with a stinging slap that sent her reeling. Her temper flared as she put a hand to her red cheek and gasped. "How dare you hit me... I'll divorce you, yes I'll divorce you."

"No you won't," he replied evenly and left the flat, banging the door behind him.

She rubbed moisturising cream into her stinging skin and stared bitterly at the imprint of his hand. Her left eye was bruised and swollen. 'This can't go on,' she thought, the tears spilling from her eyes. 'I must get away... He's a brute, and I'm afraid of him.'

Shimon, when he returned late that night was contrite. "Ettie, I'm so sorry. I don't know what came over me. Will you forgive me?" His dark imploring eyes bored into her.

She realised wearily that she was slowly becoming a battered wife. Where would it all lead to? Where could it lead to? Only separation and then divorce.

For a few weeks Shimon made a concerted effort to be with his wife more. They drove to Jaffa in the cab, wandered through the lanes, inspected the paintings and handicrafts in the galleries. "I'll buy you a painting, when I have some money..." he promised. They bought pitas at Aboulafiyas and drove home munching on the warm, fresh bread.

They made love, but her heart wasn't in it and he could feel her passivity. "It's like fucking an iceberg..." he commented after he came. She didn't reply and he withdrew his limp penis, turned round and fell asleep. She lay in the dark, her eyes wide open. Within minutes he was snoring and she grit her teeth, knowing that it would be hours before she would find relief in her dreams.

When the baby died at fifteen months and its sad little body was buried beneath a mound of earth and stones, and after sitting shiva, there seemed nothing left for her in Givataiyim and her thoughts turned more and more to the possibility of divorcing Shimon. She erred in talking to his family about it and again he turned his wrath upon her by beating her severely. She was left with both eyes badly swollen and bruised. She hid behind her sunglasses for days, but was sure that everyone could see the changing colour under her eyes. Shimon didn't come back and she still didn't confide in anyone. She felt shame... 'Me, Ettie Davidi a battered wife... No one would believe it back home. I would hate Josh ever to hear about it.' She moved out and went to live with a friend from Ulpan days, but was fearful in case he came to find her at work.

A week went by and she decided to take her salary out of their joint account, but to her dismay she discovered that he had withdrawn everything, and closed the account. She was left in dire financial straits. She borrowed from her boss to tide her over, and with his help she approached a lawyer. Shimon, however, seemed to have disappeared. His taxi was being worked by his brother, who stonily told her that he had gone away and that he hadn't left a forwarding address.

She went back to the flat but the lock had been changed and when she brought a locksmith to open the door, she discovered an empty flat devoid of furniture. Shocked and angry she turned to leave, then noticed a few letters in the box. I'll read them later, she thought and put them into her bag. Within days she realised that he had had the effrontery to sell the flat using the power of attorney she had given him.

When she finally remembered the letters, she was surprised to find one from Josh, telling her that he would be coming to Tel-Aviv the following week on business. Her heart quickened. 'How good that he should come just when I'm at my lowest.' She looked at the date on the letter. 'Heavens,' she thought, 'this is the week,' and she looked again. 'Hell, he's here at the Dan Hotel and has probably been trying to get me at the flat.'

She was pleased at his joy when he saw her and they embraced. She had planned to keep her woes to herself. Her pride had been badly hurt, but it was difficult not to break down, in his arms, and the tears flowed down her cheeks. He looked at her gravely, at her gauntness. He'd never seen her so thin before. He kissed her tearstained face, soothing her and when she had regained her composure she looked at him with shining eyes.

"Oh Josh, will you ever forgive me for what I did to you? Let's get back together again."

He looked stricken and avoided her gaze. "What is it, Josh? Tell me, please."

"Come, let us go to the Brasserie for dinner and we can talk."

They caught up on news. She questioned him about family and friends.

"Did you ever go back to Skoenesville?" she asked at last.

"Once... hell, what a dump. They built a new township about twenty miles from the place. The gold deposits were richer there and when the mines started, the Government decided to build a modern town with all amenities rather than develop Skoenesville. Many of the inhabitants, sold up and moved to Regskom."

"Who went... who stayed?"

"The Venters: remember they bought our house. Well they sold at a profit early on and, well, I suppose they had foresight. You should have seen them... Hell, they built a place you could be happy to find in Lower Houghton in Johannesburg."

"Well we certainly did them a favour," commented Ettie, "if nothing else."

"You heard about Sharpville... What a tragedy. Some of the old crowd were in gaol without trial. I got quite involved and that's where I met..." He hesitated.

"Met whom?" Ettie asked absently. Her mind was on the news she'd just heard.

"Oh the whole crowd... Slovo, Tambo... you name them. I met them, worked with them."

"Josh do be careful. You know how dangerous politics can be and it could lead..."

"Don't worry Ettie, I'm a very small cog in a big wheel... of no importance really." He wiped his lips with his serviette and took her hand in his. His eyes softened. "I was so sorry to hear about the baby. Are you trying to have another? You should, you know."

"Josh, darl," she gulped. "Not now. Could we go to your room and talk? I have so much to tell you."

"Yes, if you've finished. You won't have a coffee?" He called for the bill, and when the waiter brought over the tray, he signed and they made their way towards the lifts.

The hotel thronged with tourists and Ettie knew that it would be easier to talk in private. She was sure she wouldn't be able to control the tears, and who needed dozens of inquisitive eyes looking on.

Josh opened the door and stood aside to let her in. She turned and pulled him towards her breathlessly. Her arms went round his neck and she pressed herself close to him. Their lips found one another and she felt she'd come home at last.

She began unbuttoning his shirt, and struggled with the straps of her dress. He seemed caught up and then suddenly drew away, holding both her hands firmly in his.

"Wait Ettie... let us talk." His eyes avoided hers. He let go of her hands and pulled her straps up over her shoulders.

"Sit down here on the sofa..." He pulled her down next to him.

She watched him, loving him. 'He hasn't changed, my Josh. He still loves me and because of Shimon... he doesn't know Shimon and I have parted... he doesn't know anything at all.'

"Your news now," he said watching her. "How's Shimon... your husband?"

"We're divorcing... if I can find him, otherwise I'll be an *aguna*, a deserted wife, and will never be able to marry again... but we can live together again. Oh Josh why did I ever divorce you?" The tears flowed down her cheeks, as she related what had happened. She didn't spare him anything, although she hadn't meant to relate the beatings. She again felt the shame of being reduced to a battered wife and accepting it from the beginning.

Josh listened in pained silence. He took out a handkerchief and wiped her tears with a gentleness she thought never to experience again.

"Josh, let's marry again... as soon as I get my divorce."

He looked sad and when at last he spoke he did so hesitantly, choosing his words very carefully. "Ettie, ever since I left Israel, I've been hurting. I loved you... Oh I still do," he added hurriedly when he caught the question in her eyes. "I hurt so badly that I decided that the only way to continue was to pick up the pieces and, and..." He was at a loss for words.

"And what Josh?" she asked breathlessly, watching him.

"Well," he hesitated. "You see I knew that you were lost to me forever when you married, so I found... well you see... Ettie, oh Ettie," he gulped, "I got married last month, please understand... I can't... I'm already married."

A Long Way from Babylon

The burnt-out bus, riddled along its sides with bullet holes, stood solitary in the scorching desert sun, the gaping windows like sightless eyes turned on the vast expanse of nothingness. Thousands of shards of shattered glass, all jagged, some large, others fragmented into tiny pieces, lay half-covered by the shifting sands. I felt the glass crunch under my heavy army boots. Dried blood caked the charred seats, and I was overcome with such nausea that I jumped off the bus stairs so as not to desecrate the memory of the poor victims by adding my vomit to the carnage.

The hot southern wind blew sand into my face, into my eyes, my mouth, my ears. I fished into my army shirt for my dark glasses and hurriedly put them on. At least I could protect my eyes even though the lenses were criss-crossed with tiny spidery scratches. I spat a wad of grainy saliva onto the parched earth, lifted my face to the cloudless blue sky and howled. The echoes bouncing off the granite mountains reverberated back at me and I was shocked at the frightening animal cries. Had they come from me? I looked over my shoulder at the jeep and my companion. He looked aside, so as not to intrude on my pain.

Why hadn't I stopped her from going up north? I stop Ziva? No one could prevent her from doing what she wanted. She'd done this twelve-hour bus trip on a few occasions since arriving at the outpost as an army instructor. Her only surviving relative, her brother, lived on the Galilee kibbutz where they had made their home after arriving with the first wave of camp survivors. Her parents had died at Dachau.

The silence in this vast expanse of emptiness was overwhelming. A lone acacia tree, rooted in the sand had picked up blown away rags and papers on its thorns. The mountain peaks had been witness to the massacre... if only they could talk... I will shoot the fedayeen one by one when I find them. I took one last look over my shoulder before swinging myself into the jeep.

My companion was already in the passenger seat, his baggy khaki trousers and shirt covered in sand. He held his cocked rifle in readiness, but didn't say anything. Through the corner of my eye I saw him looking at me sympathetically. "Sorry if I startled you," I muttered. "Couldn't help myself."

"Here take this..." He handed me a canvas covered waterbottle. I lifted my head, and the tasteless water was suddenly sweet as it dribbled down my parched throat.

"Thanks," I said, as I revved up the engine.

We drove back the way we'd come. The trail was rough and we bumped over stones and rocks as only a four-wheel drive can. For the next two hours we travelled in silence. When the hazy blue sea came into view, my young companion turned to me. "Dr Zak, we'll get them... they can't get away with such a monstrosity."

"Yeah..." What could I say? I dropped him off at the base camp and drove on past Um Rashrash, where the ink flag had been raised only three years previously when Eilat had been liberated. I hoped there wouldn't be any patients waiting for me. After what I'd seen, I just wanted to be on my own with my pain and my sadness.

Home for me was my outpatient clinic and all I had were two sparsely furnished rooms, one for the clinic and one for my living quarters. I flung myself onto one of the two iron bedsteads and let go of my pent-up emotions. I hadn't cried like this since my childhood days in Baghdad. A long way from Babylon and yet the troubles were as acute... no, I dismissed the idea. Here at least we're in our own country... there we lived in fear of arrest, torture, hanging. Why don't I start from the beginning.

I had just qualified as a doctor and been awarded the King's prize to boot as the best medical student of that year, not that I ever received it. By then the War of Independence had broken out and with the Iraqi convoys rolling by on their way to holy jihad against the 'Zionist infidels' I suppose the authorities didn't like the idea of having to give a *Yahoudi* the prize, just as they were indecisive about enlisting us, the six Jewish doctors. We'd been shifted backwards and forwards until finally we'd finished the officers' course and been posted to the north.

I had led a sheltered childhood in a large family. We lived in the Jewish quarter with its high walls and shuttered windows against prying eyes... It hadn't always been like that. I remember quiet periods where we came and went at will. How I'd loved the mighty Tigris in those days, with its swirling, muddy waters, during the winter when we had torrential rain. In the dry, hot summers when the water receded, the vegetation-covered islands hoved into sight and I remember the joy of taking my pet lamb for walks along the banks, where I'd sit and dream as the small boats sailed by under the bridges.

I hadn't liked the thought of army service in the north of Iraq. In fact I hated the idea of army service altogether, but what could I do? I was enlisted and that was that. By the time I was posted to the Kurdish north I was a captain. It was with trepidation that I arrived in the mountainous north, only to be welcomed by the Kurdish Jewish community who took me to their hearts: many an evening I spent with the families, eating and exchanging stories around the open fires. The only trouble in this period, so far from the fear and turmoil of Baghdad, was the outbreak of smallpox, and we worked round the clock treating the sick. We never lost a single patient, I can say now with pride. They all recovered although they were pitted and scarred for life. I needed a break: I hadn't slept properly in weeks and was exhausted. Having asked for a transfer I found myself in Kirkuk for two weeks.

Kirkuk was a different kettle of fish, and I was introduced to the sophistication of parties with the diplomatic corps, the army officers and the businessmen. It wasn't really me, but it was different.

When I finally returned home after completing my army stint, I discovered just how bad things were in Baghdad. My elder sister and her husband had been arrested, when the authorities started censoring the mail arriving from Palestine. Anyone receiving a letter or even mentioned in the pages were arrested. Who writes a letter and doesn't send regards to this friend and that relative? Whole families were being arrested and tortured behind the thick prison walls. Fortunately my sister and her husband had contacts in the higher echelons of government and they were released. They had been badly frightened and my sister still has nightmares to this day. Others weren't so lucky.

The day... I remember it so clearly... that Ben Gurion proclaimed the State of Israel, the *Shurah*, or the armed self defence of the Iraqi

Zionist underground organisation, were posted in all the Jewish quarters of the city. As the convoys rolled by going to holy jihad, my family and I huddled together behind closed shutters, bent over the knobs of our wireless set trying to tune into Tel-Aviv above the whining and static. We caught snatches of Hebrew and over the noise and splutter we managed to piece together a picture of what was happening. We were jubilant, yet very afraid and worried, for ourselves and for the newly created State.

When the Government decreed that those wishing to leave Iraq should register, we all knew that trouble lay ahead, big trouble. We would lose our jobs, our bank accounts would be frozen, our property confiscated, and who knew whether they would really let us go. I was convinced that for me registration was the death knell. After all I had been in the army, had seen too much. For me it could only end in hanging in the city square.

While debating with myself, I witnessed the annual Ashura torchlight procession. It caught me unawares as I was returning home one evening. Most people had shut themselves indoors in fear of the black-clad Shi'ites and I had a few anxious moments as they passed me by. I watched them flagellating themselves, beating their chests and heads with chains while they bewailed the death of Hussein, the grandson of the prophet Mohammed who was murdered in Karbala together with a handful of his men. His followers broke away from mainstream Islam and set up the Shi'ite religion. Some of them were bleeding heavily but that was what they wanted, and who was I to offer them medical attention. They'd probably have lynched me had I done so. I decided then and there that I would leave illegally.

Once I'd made the decision, the problem was then to persuade my parents that this was the only solution. It was easier than I thought. They agreed immediately that there was no other way for me. My mother, who wasn't one to show her emotions, surprised me with her silent tears.

"Don't worry, I'll make it and the rest of you will follow eventually, I hope soon," I added carefully.

We were a group of six, four friends, my cousin Fouad and myself and we had made contact with the Jewish underground. They had asked me to pass information on the set-up of the Iraqi army when I arrived in Tehran. 'If I arrive in Tehran,' I thought, and for the first time a prickle of fear manifested itself in goose pimples on my upper arms.

I spent a few hours on El Rashid street: I had to see it for one last time. I knew that I'd never be back, unless I was caught; then I'd be behind bars and later on public display with my feet swinging too and fro. The hustle and bustle of the main business street had a fascination for me. It always had. The men spent their time in the many cafés lining the street. Hour after hour they sat smoking their narghillas, or fingering their worrybeads. I chose a café and sat down at a table.

"May Allah bless you with a good day," said a polite waiter as he cleaned the table. I ordered tea, the thick, black, sweet tea we all drank. I breathed in the sights and sounds. I thought of the sticky dundorma bubblegum ice-cream we had always loved to eat as kids, and ordered some, along with the tea, although hot and cold didn't mix. So what... I was on a last nostalgic visit to my favourite haunts, so I could indulge myself.

"Begging a thousand pardons..." The waiter had inadvertently spilt some of the tea as he set it down on the table.

"No matter," I hurriedly said. I didn't want to attract any untoward attention.

It wasn't easy getting away. My mother kept remembering something else. "Zak, did you take enough warm clothing? Oh and have you tied the money belt tight enough... or have you enough underwear?" What the hell do I need enough underwear for, where I'm going. We had decided to take the bare minimum with us, one small battered suitcase each, crammed with the bare necessities, so as not to arouse suspicion. I also carried an innocuous shopping bag with food for the next couple of days.

I said my goodbyes, amidst hugs and tears and wishes for Godspeed. "Don't worry," I told my parents and siblings. "We'll meet in *Eretz* Israel, soon I hope."

"Don't forget to write as soon as you arrive, son," called Mother, her lined, careworn face expressing her love and concern. I'd have to write via a friend in London and who knew whether they would ever get the letter, but I didn't remind her.

We took the night train to Basra and the journey was uneventful. For thirty-six hours we were hidden in a shack outside town, and then on a moonless night we were told to get moving as quickly and as silently as possible. The blackness of the night made the going almost impossible. We stumbled and cursed, as we followed the guide, and before long were all hidden under sacking on the rowboats. It was stifling under the sacking but we dared not lift the covering in case we were being followed.

The slap-slapping of the water against the wooden boats was reassuring, and I tried projecting my thoughts elsewhere so that I could forget the feeling of suffocation and the perspiration trickling down my neck, under my arms... I was wet through. I imagined myself back home on a starry night, on the roof, where we all slept in summer. The houses were hot and oppressive from the sweltering heat throughout the day and the only relief we had was to sleep on the roof where at night the cooler breeze blew in from the desert. I could almost taste the chilled watermelon and the cold cucumbers, the *sambousak*... all my favourite foods.

We were ordered to jump onto the river bank and follow Mahmoud, our Beduin guide, and again we stumbled in our haste to keep up. I don't know how long we walked... but as the sky slowly lightened we came to a stop and were shocked and disconcerted to find that Mahmoud had disappeared and in his place was a shifty-eyed Arab called Jumah, his black robes concealing a muscular body. He led us to a Beduin encampment and when daylight broke we were well hidden in one of their tents. We dozed uneasily throughout the day, taking it in turns to keep watch.

At nightfall, after eating a little, we set out again. We found that our suitcases were surprisingly lighter. In the pitch-black night our apprehension grew as guides changed with frequency. Someone was sure to give us away... Travel in the dark, under a moonless sky was difficult. The terrain was rocky and we stumbled again and again. We were bruised and bleeding when we came to our daylight hiding place, again a Beduin camp.

The second day passed uneventfully and we slept soundly, exhausted after the long night's travel. After eating *jaradok* and a little rice, we set out, again with a different guide. Now our cases were suspiciously lighter, but there was no time to unstrap them and check inside. I knew this area. It was mountainous. I'd been here before under such very different circumstances. This time we had donkeys to ride and the going was easier. Again we changed guides and as one disappeared another took over.

On the third day we managed to inspect our suitcases and discovered to our chagrin that everything other than our trousers had disappeared. The Beduin had no use for trousers under their *abaiyas*.

It had been an arduous three nights' journey, but we finally made the border late on the third night. As we prepared to slip over, there was a cry of "Halt... who goes there?"

Our blood curdled and we froze in our tracks. I was convinced that the Iraqi army had been tipped off and I could already feel the noose slipping around my neck.

"Zak, what do we do? Let's run for it... I'd rather be shot than go to prison and..." whispered Fouad in my ear.

"Shhhhh..." I heard the soldiers conversing and realised that they were Persian soldiers. We might make it yet.

We were taken to a hut and interrogated. The soldiers were courteous and offered us hot tea, which we accepted with gratitude, and not without a little apprehension. Would they let us go or turn us over to the Iraqis? An hour later we were pointed in the direction of Ahwaz, not before we'd given our last guide the password, who on delivering it back in Baghdad would be paid the second half of the smuggling price. At least our families would know that we'd made it.

The chill of autumn was in the air when we arrived in Tehran. We were delegated to the tent encampment in the old Jewish cemetery while we waited for our laissez-passer. Then winter crept up on us and it was hell being snowbound in a tent, but we were free. We even borrowed equipment and tried a little skiing for the first time.

We knew it would take time to get a laissez-passer, but we hadn't reckoned on three whole months before we could start moving. We six were attached to a family of ten, and were flown out as one big happy family.

The first few days in Israel passed as though in a dream. I stayed with an old business acquaintance of my father's while I looked for a job. I was lucky to find a temporary one at Beilinson Hospital and there I shared a room with an English doctor, and spent the next nine months getting to know the country.

There weren't enough army doctors and I was quickly enlisted and promised an army job in Holon if I did a three month stint in the southernmost point of the map. The place was still no more than an outpost with a few hundred hardened men and a handful of women: the men from the Engineering Corps, the army and a few pioneers. A group had just arrived from Holland with the idea of setting up a kibbutz in the Arava, but had settled for Eilat instead when they'd seen the extraordinary red of the mountains reflected in the sea at sunset.

It was like being in an oven when I arrived. The heat was overwhelming but I went straight to the beach and, fully clothed, immersed myself in the clear blue waters. The rest of the community were there having come directly from work in their shorts and *jebuti*-clad feet. Some even managed to walk over the burning sand and stones barefooted.

It didn't take me long to organise myself in my clinic, a two-roomed building with a zinc roof and an outside toilet. It was really sparsely furnished but it was home and I was free... free... free. It was 1952 and Solel Boneh had just constructed a dozen or so similar buildings next to my clinic; amongst them their offices, a bakery, a fishmeal enterprise belonging to Hamashbir Hamercazi, and a *Tnuva* café.

I wished that the rest of my family could have been as satisfied as I. They had arrived a few months previously with the mass exodus and were still bewildered and shocked at their reception. To our horror they and the rest of the immigrants, men, women and children, had been sprayed with DDT on arrival and put up in tent cities: the *maabarot* on the outskirts of Tel-Aviv. I had visited them there, helping them to settle in, and it had rained the following week – the first rains heralding the start of winter – and the sandy encampment had turned into a muddy mire. The only compensation for the rains and the beginnings of winter weather would be the disappearance, for a time anyhow, of the scorpions and the snakes which had plagued the *maabara* inhabitants those first few days.

Who would have thought winter was approaching? Here in Eilat the only relief to the dry desert heat was to immerse oneself in the sea as much as possible. Later the nights began to get cool, then cold: the desert chill which seeps into your bones. The contrast between day and night began to take its toll and I had patients lining up at the clinic, mostly with the sniffles, and the usual dysentery from the seepage in the inadequate, rusty water pipes.

The water supply to the outpost was an ongoing concern to us all. The pipes had been brought from Haifa and Ethiopia and had evidently been discarded there. They were most inadequate and were laid out from Beer Ora to the outpost, about thirty kilometres in all. However, when the water level in the well fell, the pump was left in mid-air and Eilat was left without water. We had to wait for the flight from Tel-Aviv to bring us tanks of water. It was sheer hell when that happened. The Engineering Corps worked non-stop trying to improve our lot. In the end we had Mekorot take over the water works and things improved slightly.

It was just such a situation which changed my life. Whilst we were waiting for the dakota to land with our water supply – it was a Thursday, hot as hell – we lined the airstrip with our jerrycans, tanks and waterbottles and waited impatiently in the scorching sun. It was here that I first met Ziva. She'd recently come down as an army instructor. We got talking and within days she'd moved in with me.

The sun pored in through the window sending out shafts of tiny dancing lights. The wet sheet we'd used to cover ourselves with when we'd fallen asleep was now bone dry. I felt for Ziva... she was still fast asleep and I watched her rising and falling chest. Her dark hair had fallen over her face. I contemplated getting up. Today is Shabbat and we can spend the whole day in the water. I stretched, careful not to wake her, but the sudden and urgent knocking did what I'd been careful not to do. She opened her eyes in alarm as I made for the door, tying a towel round my waist.

"Dr Zak... Dr Zak Artzi?"

"Yes... what is it?" I asked the young soldier. I hadn't seen him before. He must be a newcomer. He put out his arm and I was confronted with a patch of angry redness and swelling under the wiry blond hairs. Jericho rose, I thought. I haven't seen this since leaving Iraq. I looked at him. "It's not a bite... You'll need some treatment for this, and you may be left with a scar, but it'll be all right." I reassured him.

Shabbat or no Shabbat, when folks are sick they have to be attended to. That's what I'm here for, anyway, I thought, as two more patients appeared. I treated the dysentery patient and then looked at Marta, her distended stomach was low...

"Are you sure you're not in your ninth month?" I asked her, after examining her.

"No, Dr Zak," she protested. "I'm beginning my eighth month, but the pains have been coming for the last hour."

"Shouldn't you have been flying soon to the north?"

She nodded. "Yes, I had planned to do so next Thursday and stay with my parents in Petach Tikve. They're near the Beilinson hospital."

I had told her a month ago to make preparations to go. The outpost was no place to give birth. If there were any complications I was ill equipped to deal with them... God, how had I miscalculated as I had? I began to perspire heavily. If it was straightforward everything would be fine, but if not...

"Don't worry, Marta, it'll be all right, as long as you do exactly as I tell you. Here, come lie down in the clinic."

Ziva was on hand and she boiled up some water and spread out the towels. Her black eyes were troubled. She said nothing to Marta but she whispered to me outside. "Zak, have you ever delivered a baby before?"

"Of course I have..." I was indignant. I hadn't though under such circumstances, and I could only hope for the best.

Instead of spending our leisure day in the water, Ziva and I, Marta and her husband spent the day waiting. Between contractions we managed to down a couple of coffees. Ziva kept wetting sheets to cool the woman, but they dried so quickly. We opened all the windows and doors, anything for a through breeze, but to no avail. It was towards sunset that Marta finally gave birth to a boy, the first baby born in Eilat in two thousand years. Most of the inhabitants crowded outside the door in excitement. I was lucky... we were both lucky... no, all three lucky. The birth was uncomplicated.

During the week, excitement mounted as preparations were made for the first *Brit Milah*, and when the old man announced that he would be coming down, excitement reached a feverish pitch.

On the eighth day after the birth, all the civilians and the army were at the airstrip when the dakota landed. Ben Gurion, his wife Paula, dignitaries and notables alighted to much fanfare and clapping. They were taken on a quick tour of the outpost and then the old man acted as godfather, as the baby was circumcised.

I was thrilled to meet Israel's first prime minister in person. We talked for some time about developing the Arava. He was an enthusiastic advocate of settling people in the desert and cultivating the land.

For the first time I was caught in an embarrassing situation. The old man insisted I join them for photographs. "Young man," he said, his eyes twinkling. "You should be proud to have delivered the first baby here in a millennium. You and the baby have made history."

Next day Ziva announced that she was going up to visit her brother and would be away for about a week. I drove her to the bus station and saw her onto the bus.

"I'll miss you Ziva... come back as soon as possible."

She smiled and leaned over to kiss me. 'She is so beautiful,' I thought. 'How lucky I am that with all these unattached men, she chose me.'

The bus was already out of view. Only the dust from the wheels remained and that settled down quickly. I started up the jeep and drove back to the clinic. 'It will be lonely without Ziva,' I thought. 'I'll just have to spend more time reading. Still she'll be back before the holidays. I think we should get married...' I startled myself with those thoughts. I wondered whether she would accept my proposal. She said she loved me but she also never spoke much about herself. 'Well I can ask her...' my heart pumped wildly and I looked forward impatiently to her return.

The shocking news came the following day. The bus had been ambushed and most of the passengers slaughtered. There had been a couple of survivors; no one knew yet who the lucky few were and we waited for news. Names were not being released yet, not until all the victim's families had been contacted. I and the rest of the outpost inhabitants were unable to work, unable to function. We sought one another's company. We tried calling army authorities, but to no avail.

On the second day the haggard citizens were informed one by one who'd lost relatives. The outpost was in mourning and as the names were read out people fainted, wept or remained silent with wide, haunted eyes. I waited in shock as one name followed another. I knew them all. They were either friends or patients or relatives of the outpost inhabitants... people who'd come to visit. The voice droned on and as I held my breath I heard, "Ziva Levi..."

My world crumbled around me. My mouth was dry and I was numb with horror. Someone touched my elbow. "Zak I'm so sorry." I nodded and moved slowly away. There was time to offer my condolences to the others. Right now I had to be alone.

I walked along the water's edge kicking up sand and pebbles, my eyes downcast. I had at long last found someone to settle down with and I'd lost her... why hadn't I prevented her from going? 'I couldn't have prevented her, so don't be ridiculous,' I told myself. I hurt so badly. I felt as though someone had put a dagger into my chest and started to twist. The pain was unbearable and the tears flowed freely. I must have walked for hours because the sun had begun to settle in the west and the hills behind me were darkening.

The clinic... I suddenly remembered. I probably had patients waiting for me and as I was the only doctor for civilians and army alike, I wasn't being fair. There had been others bereaved too... how could I have been so irresponsible?

One of the men, Moshe it was, sat on the only chair, his eyes pensive. He jumped up when he saw me. "Dr Zak, I didn't want to disturb you so I dealt with the few patients who were waiting for you. Is that OK?"

I was alarmed... how had he dealt with them? What medical experience did he have? Nothing as far as I knew.

"I did a basic nursing course in Tel-Aviv for a couple of months..." he ended lamely.

"How did you treat the patients?" I asked him.

He gave me a rundown, two men with superficial wounds he'd swabbed with disinfectant and bandaged. To a third, he'd given a tranquilliser pill.

"Thanks Moshe..." I pressed his shoulder in gratitude. I shouldn't have doubted him. He had done it for me.

It was not until I'd been to the scene of the massacre that I was able to accept that Ziva really was dead. I had let out my pain in that mighty howl which must have echoed for miles around. I wasn't to be left with my thoughts for very long before being brought back to the present by urgent knocking.

"Dr Artzi, Dr Zak, this just came for you." I took the note from the young soldier: 'Three kids caught and shot in Petra. We want you to come to the border and collect the bodies.' They had crossed the border into enemy territory on their way to the Nabatean city hewn into the red rock. It seemed to happen every few months or so, although this was the first time I had been called to collect the bodies. Many had been killed before they got there and even this didn't seem to deter the others. Very few had escaped alive and those who did became heroes amongst their peers. I groaned. "I'll be with you in a moment."

We drove along the stony beach, a couple of command cars following us. The tide had turned and had left the watermark halfway up the sand. The tires of the command cars crunched on the pebbles and spewed up sand.

The sun was beginning its descent and a hot wind blew into our faces. Most of the population were in the water cooling off after a long day's work which started at three or four in the morning and ended when the heat was unbearable.

"Sorry you have to go through all this," mumbled my driver, embarrassed. "Especially after..."

I nodded. What was there to say?

When we came to the battered 'Halt – Frontier ahead' sign, the soldiers already there moved the barbed-wire barrier and we drove into no man's land. The command cars stood in line and the silent soldiers, their faces impassive, watched as I walked towards the three stretchers. I bent down and uncovered the first body.

Pity and anger welled up inside me. What a waste of three young lives. I looked at the pale, freckled face under the mop of ginger hair. What had prompted these kids to go, and how did this poor boy think he could get away with it looking as he did? I examined the other two and then nodded to the soldiers as I straightened up. The procedure hadn't taken five minutes, but I felt drained.

We drove back the way we came and I folded my arms so that my driver wouldn't see my shaking hands. Ziva must have looked like that in death. I imagined her face peaceful yet pale, her black hair swept up into a knot, the wisps of untidy hair framing those expressive black eyes now closed for all eternity. I hadn't heard from her brother, although I'd written.

There was a commotion on the beach and we could see the crowds in the distance. As we neared, my driver muttered, "Palamidas."

The fishermen were pulling in dozens of gasping flapping fish and the crowds were stuffing them into buckets, basins, pots, in fact any available container.

"Are we going to be eating fish for the rest of the month?" I asked in amazement.

"Only tonight..." My driver turned to me with a smile. "Once a year we have these palamida invasions. We don't know the reason for this but we make good use of it."

"*Kumzitz* tonight," someone yelled. "Dr Zak you will come won't you?"

"Thanks, yes." I was grateful for the invitation. At least it would take my mind off the tragedies, for a short time at least.

Lack of sleep and the events of the past few weeks had taken a toll on me. I tumbled into bed, my baggy shorts still wet from the late afternoon swim. I must have fallen into a deep sleep.

The ear-splitting roar of the landing dakota... only I didn't know then that it was the weekly plane, came exactly as the bullets rained down on us. Ziva and I were in a canyon, the granite mountains towering above us. The roar was deafening, as the bullets rained from all sides.

"Down Ziva..." I yelled, pulling her to the ground and covering her with my body. The perspiration poured off me and I felt for my gun... damn, someone stole it while we were asleep. Ziva didn't stir although the bullets kicked up the earth around us, covering us with red, green, yellow and blue sand. 'How strange,' I thought, 'and how colourful. Oh God, she's not breathing.' I rolled off her in panic and turned her face. Her eyes were wide open in fear and blood dribbled out the side of her mouth.

"You bastards!" I screamed. "You've killed her. Ziva, don't die, I'll get you to hospital. Ziva, wake up, please wake up."

"Zak, wake up... Zak."

The noise had died down and I was suddenly aware that someone was shaking my shoulder.

"Thank God you're safe, Ziva... Have the bastards gone?"

"What bastards?" she asked me teasingly.

I jumped out of bed. Was I dreaming? Yes, I had been dreaming. Ziva was dead. No, she was alive. I paced the floor swinging my arms and slapping my shoulders. 'Must wake up no matter how hard it is,' I thought.

I turned round. She was still there. She sat quietly looking up at me. I saw loving pity in her eyes but there was a slight smile on her lips. "Zak, come sit down next to me." She patted the bed, smoothing the bed sheets. "I wasn't on that bus... Yes, there was a Ziva Levi. She was coming down to Eilat for the first time."

"Ziva, Ziva... It really is you?" I held her in my arms and we rocked to and fro, our tears mingling.

"I was sent on a mission; never mind what." She put a finger to my lips. "When I got back to the kibbutz, I found the letter you sent to my brother: he's been away. In fact he still hadn't returned when I arrived. Well, I recognised your handwriting so I opened it. It was only then that I realised that a dreadful mistake had been made, so I flew down on today's flight. Zak, I'm so sorry... so very sorry."

A cheer went up outside the door. We hadn't been aware of the crowds collecting outside. Some of the men had seen Ziva arriving and the news had spread like wildfire. Many eyes were moist as they watched us, and I, I had an indescribable feeling of joy.

A Decent Burial

Those Thanksgiving dinners at my grandparents' house were the highlight of my adolescent years. A couple of weeks before the trip my parents would inevitably get into the usual argument.

"This year we're staying home for Thanksgiving and that's that," Dad would say firmly.

"Hon, you know we can't let my parents down, it's all they live for, our annual trip up to see them. I know Daddy is tiresome, but it's only for a couple of days," Mom would say persuasively. When she 'Honned' you knew she wasn't giving in. She always got her way in the end, being very organised and very determined.

I seemed to be the only one who looked forward to the trip. Grandad liked fishing. It was one of the only things he did like, that and baseball, although I suspected that he liked me in his way. He sure had an odd way of showing it though. He complained bitterly about my messiness: my hair was too long. "Get the boy to cut it," he'd growl. I was spoilt as an only child, he contended, and there were still no signs I was growing up to be a man. So why did I suspect he had a soft spot for me? If Mom or Dad told me off for something, he would stand up for me.

"Leave the boy alone," he'd say protectively. "Boys will be boys, and he's OK."

The fishing was great and on good days we'd bring our catch home in elation, yet still full of talk of the one, the big one that got away. November was bitingly cold and although we always dressed warmly on these outings, as soon as we were out of sight of the house and Grandma's watchful eyes, Grandad invariably discarded his oil-streaked fleece-lined jacket which had seen better days, leaving his gloves; the latter of which had the tops of the fingers cut off. "All the better with which to feel the rod and the fish," he'd explain. I learned much about baseball, the stars, the tides, the assortment of river, lake and sea life. Grandad was quite a raconteur once he was out on the water, and I loved his stories.

He was an impressive looking man, large, with greying hair and ice-blue eyes which lightened his deeply etched sunburnt face. He had been the quintessential sportsman in his day, hunting deer, playing tennis and representing his college in athletics. Some days we'd go out in the rowboat, others we'd stand on the landing.

Most of the great maples were starkly bereft of their leaves, although a few still had the remains of yellows, golds and russets, but these leaves too fluttered slowly earthwards one by one, seeming loath to part from their strategic vantage points from which the world was theirs.

My Dad wasn't interested in fishing. In fact his interests didn't encompass sports in any way at all. He taught literature and creative writing at the local college. He wore tweed jackets and chewed a pipe. Mom thought he looked like an Oxford don and not like an American associate professor. His eyes behind thick lenses were always in some book or newspaper, his attention so completely absorbed in what he was reading that we'd have to repeat ourselves umpteen times before he'd hear us.

Dad never spoke about himself. I knew very early on that his parents and sister had died, but we were never allowed to mention them. Mom was an only child and so it seemed that we were a family of one set of grandparents, parents and myself. I never saw Dad put his foot in a church, not that we went regularly but I remember a couple of occasions where Mom and Grandma insisted on my coming. They were both sticklers for doing the right thing, and fine manners and discipline were most important to them, in fact the ruling axioms of their lives.

The first great upheaval in my life came when Grandma died suddenly. We drove up to New England for the cremation. I pretended to have stomach cramps so that I wouldn't have to be at the ceremony. Mom gave me some ghastly tasting white powder dissolved in water to calm me down and I sat between dry-eyed Dad and weeping Mom. Grandad sat ramrod straight and although he looked bad he didn't say a word.

I remember the white lilies, the candles, the mahogany coffin... they had discussed the mahogany. There were quite a few people there, many I hadn't seen before and everyone came over to shake our hands and murmur their condolences. I must have been about twelve at the time so I don't remember too much about it other than I kept my eyes tightly shut when the coffin slid slowly out of sight to be consumed by the flames.

Thanksgiving was still a few months away, but we left Mom with Grandad for a few days. She came back very subdued and I overheard her telling Dad that Grandma had taken her place alongside the porcelain figurines on the mantelpiece.

Imagine my discomfort when we next drove up to Grandad's for the Thanksgiving vacation and found Grandma's remains in a bronze urn on the mantel. When we sat down to the mouth-watering turkey Mrs Forbes the temporary cook had prepared, Grandad brought the urn into the dining room and set it down on a side table. He clasped his hands, lowered his head and said grace. We three dutifully mouthed our Amens. He then looked at me. "Grandma is with us and will always be with us," he said gruffly at my wide eyed questioning. I could hardly swallow. "What's wrong with the boy?" Grandad asked. "He doesn't seem to have his usual hearty appetite this year."

I was chosen for the school basketball team the year I turned sixteen. Dad wasn't impressed. "I wish you'd spend more time on your books and less on sport," he'd commented, emphasising his expectations of me, the impact of which seemed to bounce off me leaving only my reflection in his lenses. I knew I was a disappointment to him, as I, the offspring of one from the higher echelons of the educational hierarchy, was expected to deliver, but my grades weren't too good. I daydreamed through maths, history, geography and the rest. At one of the practices I collided with one of the opposite team.

"Jeez sorry."

"Jew bastard..." he muttered. I was puzzled. I'd never heard anyone make such derogatory statements before, and why to me?

"I said I was sorry," I repeated.

"Sorry?" he yelled at me. "You'll be sorrier yet when I've finished with you, you circumcised scumbag."

There was self-conscious laughter in the background, and I limped off the court in a fury. This was my first introduction to anti-Semitism, though at that stage I didn't even know anything about it.

"I was called a Jew bastard and a circumcised scumbag today at practice," I mentioned later to Dad, still smarting at the insult but worst of all the laughter.

He said nothing but hunched his shoulders and buried his nose further in the book he was reading. Mom had overheard and she went pale and pursed her lips. "What did you do about it?" she asked, staring at me.

"I ignored it, but I would like to know what it's all about."

"It's blatant anti-Semitism... that's what." Dad's voice was flat and he didn't take his eyes off the book.

"Well we're not Jewish, although over the years people have asked me whether I am." I admitted, wondering for a moment why.

Neither of my parents said anything further. They just simply didn't like to discuss anything very much with me. Even my questions about sex at the age of eleven had been brushed aside. There were certain subjects that were taboo in our house. Well I'd read up about sex and the practical part of my sexual education I'd got at fifteen when Samantha Parkhurst had let me feel her up. That was at the MacLean twins' birthday party, and we'd slipped out into the garden right behind the greenhouse. She had shown me what a French kiss was and I sure liked it. I was ready to French kiss for ever after. Her boobs were nice too, sort of melony, the small round ones that is. That's as far as we'd got then.

I'd lie on my bed listening to albums of Elvis... I wondered idly whether I should take up the sax, and thought of Samantha. I always had a hot feeling when I thought of her. Elvis... most of my walls were plastered with pictures of Elvis, also James Dean; after the Samantha interlude Marilyn Monroe joined them, looking down on me from her plastered heights.

Conversation at the dinner table had always been pretty boring and as the years went by we three continued to talk at a tangent. Dad was interested in politics... and books of course and the Kennedy administration, the civil rights movement, the riots in Little Rock Arkansas, the Bay of Pigs. I was only superficially aware of these events from the discussions. My interests lay in the World Series, and when the Yankees won for the twenty-sixth time I was in seventh heaven.

Mom's enthusiasm for the society pages of the newspapers and magazines was an eternal source of irritation to Dad. He'd be upset by Ernest Hemingway's suicide and she'd bring up the subject of the Boston party thrown by the O'Shaughnessys. Was it Sean or Sir Patrick... what difference, they were both there with their young French wives... sisters, both Contessas...

I began to take an interest in Judaism when I saw the coverage of the trial of the Nazi war criminal Adolf Eichman, in Israel. I read avidly and was horrified at what I read. I wondered whether I should talk to Dad about what I'd learnt.

I found him sitting hypnotised in front of the TV one evening as the trial's progress was reported. We began talking and I was surprised at Dad's extensive knowledge of the Holocaust. He gave me titles of books to read and I devoured them all. I read about Israel and the more I read the more I identified with the Jews. How I wished I was Jewish. I never dared wish aloud. My parents would have been shocked.

I was at college in my senior year and was about to use a much needed break from the books and take my date to the drive-in, when Mom phoned, weeping, to say that Dad had had a stroke. Mom and I spent hours at the hospital while he hovered on a thread between life and death. Mom cried a great deal and prayed to God that He should spare her darling Mort. "He's only fifty-three... it's too soon for him to go," she wept.

I was in the middle of orals, and there was no way that I would be able to concentrate on study. I was fed up with college and knew that I wanted out, but once out I also knew I'd be drafted. Perhaps I should join the marines, I thought fleetingly. The beginning of the school year had been disrupted by the assassination. Dad had taken it badly; we all had, but he'd been very pro-Kennedy, and he and Mom had spent days discussing the tragedy, he from the political repercussions and she from the "So young and beautiful and already a widow with two small children" point of view.

Dad died in the early morning of 7th May and it was like my world fell apart around me. Mom and I argued about the cremation. I felt he should have a decent burial, but she was firm in her resolve to cremate him. I gave in, but begged her not to put Dad's remains in an urn, on the mantel.

"Darling," she said sadly, her eyes moist. "We will all in turn be cremated and placed in an urn. You can bury my urn, when my time comes, together with your father's urn, or keep them with you if you like. No, I see you don't. Well there is a family mausoleum where all the urns will eventually be buried and you will be able to do it for us. Until then Morty stays with me."

Thanksgiving of that year I drove Mom and the urn in the old Chevvy, up to Grandad's, and Dad's and Grandma's urns graced the side table while we ate our Thanksgiving turkey. Again I wasn't able to eat and resolved that this would be my last Thanksgiving at Grandad's. I wasn't sure what I was going to do. I had flunked a couple of exams, not all of them, but Mom had been most upset when I'd informed her that I was dropping out of school. An alternative was the army or the marines. I would no doubt be drafted very soon, especially if I was no longer studying. I didn't mind joining up but I wanted to travel first and what I really had set my heart on was a trip to Israel. Perhaps I could volunteer to work on a kibbutz.

It was a cold and wet day in December when I landed at the Lod airport and as I had only a backpack which was first off the baggage roundabout, I was through customs and on my way to Tel-Aviv in no time at all. The cab driver was surprisingly talkative: where was I from, how old was I, what did I intend doing, what did my father do, how much had he earned at the University? This was all so foreign to me, coming from a background where one didn't ask interminable questions, certainly not of a stranger... in fact didn't ask questions, full stop. I liked this introduction to a country teeming with noise, hospitality, warmth and friendliness. I didn't seem to notice anything that wasn't positive about the place, the babble of dozens of different strange tongues, the intermixing of displaced peoples from the four corners of the earth. Here, I thought, was a pluralist society where all peoples could co-exist. There was an excitement in the air: the joy of being young in a country struggling to rebuild on ancient foundations.

I quickly found my feet and after trekking through the length and breadth of the country - not very wide - I decided to try a kibbutz. We were a small group of volunteers from Australia, South Africa, France and Italy, in fact six of us in all. I was 'adopted' by a veteran couple, Yaakov and Miriam, who'd been through the depths of hell and survived. They had managed to rescue their two children from the inferno in the late thirties by sending them on *aliyah* to Palestine, but they themselves hadn't been lucky enough to get out in time. They had finally been united with their children after the war only to lose their son in the War of Independence. The daughter had married a man from a neighbouring kibbutz, so they weren't too far from their two grandchildren.

They were warm, concerned and caring people and I would spend many an hour in deep conversation with them. There wasn't a subject that was considered taboo with them, and I wished again and again that my own parents had been like that. Miriam had heavy pendulous breasts which she hid under her housecoat or loose fitting shirts, and her constant concern for us all made her a typical Yiddishe Mama, as Yaakov would say lovingly.

I picked up the lingo pretty fast and within three months was already speaking Hebrew. The thing is I wasn't embarrassed to try out my Hebrew as some of my fellow volunteers were, and everyone took delight in correcting me, to my advantage of course.

I worked in the orange groves where we picked oranges from dawn to midday. At about seven in the morning the tractor would arrive bearing our breakfast of white cheese, olives, tomatoes, fresh bread or pita and, best of all, halvah. The sweet halvah disappeared under tens of outstretched hands, but after the first few days where I wasn't quick enough and the treat was gone before I even got to it, I learned to elbow and push with the best of them. We sang and sweated as we worked.

Lessons were in the afternoon and our evenings were spent mingling with the kibbutz members. After my stint in the groves I took my turn doing kitchen and dining room duty. It also had its advantages. At least on the many scorching *sharav* days I was under a roof, but just as hot and sweaty. I learned to cook, to wash dishes, set tables... I approved of the *kolboynik* on each table: a plastic basin where members threw eggshells, olive pits, cigarette ash and stubs, in short a miniature garbage bin.

Evenings there were lectures, many ideological in nature, and sing-alongs where we'd sit on the grass outside the communal dining room, singing the Hebrew songs we'd learnt to the accompaniment of the accordion.

I was attracted to an olive-skinned, black-eyed beauty who worked in the baby house and at first I would wander in under the pretext that I'd come to see the children. Varda seemed to like me and in the late afternoons when the parents came to collect their kids for a few hours of family togetherness, she would join me at Miriam and Yaakov's.

Varda had come to the kibbutz as a young girl, having left Morocco with an aunt in the mid fifties. Her parents had died on the way to Israel and they hadn't seen the promised land. She still had family back in Casablanca, grandparents, uncles, aunts and cousins, and although they talked of coming to Israel, they were loath to leave a comfortable lifestyle and start from scratch. In retrospect I can say that this was a most stimulating period in my life.

With our six months of volunteering completed and me speaking a passable Hebrew I debated where to go from there. Should I remain on the kibbutz, continue my travels and then go back home? Mom and Grandad kept asking when I intended coming home; the scribbled postcards from Grandad were difficult to decipher. I guessed that Mom pushed him to write. Her letters were long and newsy in beautifully clear script.

She had sold the house and moved to Grandad's and I visualised the two of them carrying their urns into the dining room every mealtime. Surely they had stopped the practice. She had reorganised the house and was doing some charity work with the church ladies... I felt so divorced from all that was important to Mom, I didn't think I would fit into any lifestyle back home.

When February came round again, I knew for sure I wanted to stay in Israel. Not being Jewish the law of return didn't apply to me, and I had to renew my visa every few months which was a drag. I had borrowed books on Judaism from Yaakov and when I wasn't working I would read voraciously, always discussing the books with him afterwards.

He was an enigma... he had studied in a yeshiva as a young boy in Lithuania, and had come from a long line of Rabbis. Judaism for him was a way of life without the traditional rituals. "I don't need to be in synagogue to pray... I can do it at home, in the fields, in the workshop, anywhere," he'd explain.

It had been a long day. Varda and I sat on the grass outside my 'adopted' parent's home. Yaakov had been reflective for some while and we drank tea and ate the cookies Miriam had prepared. All around us was the buzz of neighbours' conversation, and the sounds of children's laughter. I lay back on the grass with my arm under my head watching the drifting clouds. I had never belonged as I did now, I mused, and yet... I sat up hurriedly. "Yaakov, I want to become

Jewish: have wanted it ever since I learned about Judaism. How do I go about it?"

Yaakov looked astonished. "Are you sure? It's no easy thing being a Jew..." he looked from me to Varda.

"No... no, don't look at me," she protested. "I had nothing to do with this decision."

I shook my head. "No, she's right, Yaakov. It has nothing to do with the fact that Varda and I are shacked up together. It's something deep inside me, something which has been growing since the day I was called a scumbag, and..."

"That's no reason..."

"Ah yes, but it is... That's when I became conscious of Judaism."

From then onwards my studies intensified. Yaakov spoke of the centuries of persecution, of the inquisition, the pogroms, the ghettos and the Holocaust. Little by little he began to relate his own experiences of the war. I had noticed the numbers branded on his and Miriam's arms when I'd first met them, so knew that they had been in the camps. He spoke of the cattle car carrying them to their destination... the gates with the 'Arbeit macht frei' over the archway to hell. The lines of naked men, women and children being directed left or right. I had read many horrifying stories of what went on, but to hear it first hand from someone who'd gone to the depths of hell and survived was harrowing for me. I relived the horrors with him. We cried together, the tears rolling down our cheeks in silence. Perhaps this was the first time he'd shed tears.

I began to study with the rabbi in Afula. He warned me that it was a long, drawn-out process and that I should have patience. "How long a process?" I asked.

"You'll be lucky if you manage in two years."

He was either being brutally honest or trying to dissuade me. 'Hell,' I thought, 'two years is too long,' but I kept silent.

For months I debated whether or not to tell Mom what I had decided. It was only when she wrote to say that she was thinking of visiting me in the fall that I finally plucked up the courage to write her about my endeavours. Better to prepare her beforehand, I thought.

Varda seemed withdrawn for the better part of a week and I wondered whether I'd done anything to upset her. One morning I found her retching over the toilet bowl.

"You must have eaten something... maybe the felafel you had in Afula yesterday?"

She shook her head, her face pale, her expressive eyes watching me silently. She seemed to be struggling with herself then, as though she'd made up her mind, she dropped the bombshell.

"I'm pregnant... second month."

I stared at her, the blood pounding in my head. There was still much I wanted to do before getting married. I was too young to be a father. Did I love Varda enough to marry her? Yes, I thought I did, but I hadn't planned to do so for some years yet.

"Don't worry," she said softly, almost reading my thoughts. I'm not asking you to marry me. In fact I don't want to get married... but I intend keeping the baby. You don't have to acknowledge paternity... in fact you can leave me right now." Her voice rose chokingly and she rushed back to the toilet.

She reappeared as though nothing had happened and the colour seemed to have returned to her cheeks. I put my arms around her but she didn't move. "Come sit down and let's talk," I said, gently propelling her towards the sofa. She sat down reluctantly and seemed about to say something.

"No... first listen to what I have to say," I said firmly. My thoughts were in turmoil and I wasn't sure what I was going to say. "I was shocked at this unexpected turn of events," I began, "so didn't react positively at first. Now that the enormity of the event has begun to sink in..."

"It was stupid of me even to tell you." She stared at me angrily.

"No Varda, it was the right thing and I'm genuinely happy." I stood up suddenly and whooped, "I'm going to be a father!" and whirled round, my face upturned, my hands outstretched. She laughed, joining me and we clasped each other and waltzed to "I'm going to be a father, one two three, one, two three..."

My kibbutz parents were delighted with the news. "Does that mean you'll stay with us and marry Varda?" Yaakov asked tentatively.

"We'll have to marry abroad in a civil marriage... and when I eventually get my conversion, we'll have a Jewish wedding."

Yaakov shook his head. "When you become a Jew, we'll give you the wedding here. The baby when born will automatically be Jewish because Varda is a Jewess... here there is no such thing as illegitimacy unless the child is conceived of a married woman by someone other than her husband, so you don't have to worry."

I wrote Mom a long letter and hoped she wouldn't try to dissuade me. I knew she had plans for me and had heard her talking over the years of the wonderful church wedding she visualised for me, with a daughter of one of the scions of New England. She still hoped I'd finish college, although her hopes for Yale or Harvard had diminished somewhat.

The telegram arrived a week later. It was from Grandad. "Your mother hospitalised after car accident. Condition serious but stable. Request return home immediately."

I hitched a ride to Afula, and found the travel agency I'd been directed to. There was a flight out the following day to New York. Before the expiry date of my return ticket some months before, I had managed to get a refund so I had to buy a new ticket. I made sure it was a return ticket. Mom would be well again in no time, I was sure. I hoped that she wouldn't be left with any disabilities. She wouldn't be able to deal with any physical handicaps. She was too much of a perfectionist in everything, even her physical being.

I said my farewells to Yaakov, Miriam and the rest of the kibbutz members. Varda was to accompany me to Lod. Hell, I sure would miss her. She was silent most of the way to the airport. I took her hand in mine and tucked it under my arm.

"Hey Varda," I said gruffly, trying to sound nonchalant. "Don't change your mind about me while I'm away."

She withdrew her hand, the hurt showing in her eyes. "How could you even think that of me. I love you stupid. Don't you know it yet?" and she burst into tears.

God, what sort of an unfeeling idiot I'd been. "Varda... I'm sorry. I shouldn't have said what I said. It's just that I love you and was uncertain of your love."

The bus came to a stop outside the departure terminal, and we alighted. I checked in. We hung around for awhile. We were loath to part. "I'll be back in no time... Look after him." I put my hand on her stomach.

She smiled wanly. "Her... sure I'll look after her."

"Whichever, I don't mind."

It was difficult to part and when I got to midway up the stairs, I could still see Varda's sad face. Then the hanging metal sign hid her from view and I made my way to passport control.

I was lucky to get the shuttle from Kennedy, in fact I just made it before the gate closed. I was dead tired and hadn't slept for at least twenty-seven hours. On arrival, I took a cab directly to the hospital and found Mom in intensive care.

"Your grandfather is in the waiting room and has been there since early this morning," explained the young nurse at reception. "Mrs Barron took a turn for the worse in the early hours of this morning. The doctors are with her, although she seems stable now."

Grandad sat hunched over, his chin cupped in his hands, his eyes focused on some inanimate object, yet I felt sure that his thoughts were miles away. I watched him for a while. He had aged terribly in the fifteen months I'd been away. I touched his shoulder lightly. "Hi Grandad, I'm here..."

He looked up at me with his pale-blue, watery eyes, for a moment not comprehending that I had arrived. Sudden recognition spurred him to rise and he struggled to pull himself up, holding on to the chair back as he stood up unsteadily. He put out a gnarled hand to shake mine and then thought better of it and took a tottering step forward and embraced me. Grandad had never done that before and although I was taken aback, I gladly returned his bearhug.

"How's Mom?" I asked anxiously.

"Sit down son... The old man lowered himself slowly onto the straight-backed chair again and I sat down on the armchair next to him. "Your mother was knocked over by a hit and run driver and she's been in a coma ever since. She's on the respirator and had been stable until early this morning."

"What are her chances Grandad?" I asked softly almost afraid to hear the answer.

"The doctors were hopeful yesterday and felt that she may be coming round. The nurse had noticed her eyelids fluttering when I spoke to her. Evidently her head took the full force of the impact as she doesn't seem to have any other internal injuries, although her body is very bruised." Grandad shook his head wearily. "I'm glad to see you and she will be too when she comes round."

I noticed that he said 'when' and not 'if', which was encouraging, and meant surely that she was out of the woods.

"When can I see Mom?"

"As soon as the doctors have done their ward rounds, the private nurse will call us... at present they're with her. A neurologist has been called in for a second opinion, as they're contemplating possible surgery."

We were silent for some time, until the nurse I'd spoken with put her head in through the doorway and said we could go in and see Mom. I was scared stiff and followed Grandad, noticing how short and how stooped he appeared.

Mom lay under hospital sheets and only her head and arms were exposed, both arms stuck with needles from which tubes wound upwards towards the intravenous bags. Mom's face was pale under the breathing apparatus. I sat down awkwardly on one side of the bed and Grandad sat on the other side.

"Talk to your mother," he instructed. "If she hears your voice, she may make a speedier recovery."

"Hi Mom it's me... I came as soon as I could and I have so much to tell you about Israel..."

Grandad frowningly shook his head. "Leave that part out... Speak only of what makes her happy. Tell her you're here for good and you're going back to college."

"No, that's not true. I'm getting..."

"Stop," commanded the old man. "Do as I tell you." He sounded so fierce that I figured he must have a reason for his demands, so 'What the hell,' I thought, 'if it helps Mom I'll acquiesce.' I nodded and began all over again. I spoke of how great it was to be back, how I'd missed her and Grandad, how I was eager to go fishing again, how I couldn't wait to taste her famous blueberry muffins.

"You know Mom, I might even go back to college and get my degree..." I looked at Grandad for approval and crossed my fingers. Why was I lying? She couldn't hear anyway, so it didn't matter really.

"Be more specific boy..." Grandad prodded me.

"Well I know Mom that you always wanted me to try for the big ones and who knows I might even get accepted if I put my mind to it. I'm ready to settle down. First true statement, I thought, only they didn't know what I meant. I suddenly remembered that I'd written Mom about my and Varda's plans. Hadn't she given the letter to Grandad to read?

As the hours went by I grew bolder and more convincing in my lies. I invented more for Mom to hear. On the third day after my arrival we thought we detected the faintest eyelid movement when I told her I was home for good, that I'd written away for application forms from a couple of the important universities I almost had myself believing myself. Grandad all the while nodded his approval.

There was no point in upsetting the old man so I kept the truth to myself and became most adept at imaginative conversation... anything to bring Mom back to this world.

Mom had modernised Grandad's house and had removed many of the old oak panels in the drawing room and in the dining room. Only the study and the library were still panelled. The two urns stood side by side in the study and Grandad had stopped the practice of carrying Grandma's urn into meals. The kitchen had been redone and my room seemed to have been moved lock, stock and barrel from the old house and transplanted into New England. Even the pictures had been removed from the old walls and repasted onto the new. I felt strange in my new old room. My tastes had changed: although I still liked Elvis and the rest, I had wider interests now.

Mom never regained consciousness but I learned a lot about her life from Grandad. We were both with her – I talking non-stop in the hope she would come to – when she suddenly stopped breathing. The nurse checked her pulse, called for help and within seconds the doctors had arrived and Grandad and I were ordered out. Ten minutes later Mom's attendant doctor gently broke the news of her death. I was stunned and Grandad seemed to shrink even further.

I had managed to cable Varda and then sat down to pen a short letter telling her that it would be a good few weeks before my return. There was quite a lot to attend to, what with the cremation, the final burial... I had persuaded Grandad that my mother's remains should be transported together with Dad's urn and put to final rest in the family mausoleum. He agreed, but under no circumstances would he part with Grandma's urn. Well, I'd have to deal with that when his time came.

The old man seemed to depend on me now. He hovered anxiously around me. "You are back for good?" he asked me one morning at breakfast, looking up from his muffins and removing his tortoiseshell glasses from his faded blue eyes.

"Grandad, didn't Mom tell you that I and Varda are getting married?"

He was silent for some moments, only his head trembled very slightly. I knew he had the beginnings of Parkinson's but it was becoming more noticeable now. He cleared his throat and spat the contents into a rumpled handkerchief he withdrew from his pocket. "Son..." he said gently. "Your mother never had the chance to tell me. The accident happened after she received your letter. When she was knocked down, she still clutched the pages and the attendant at the hospital gave me the letter when I arrived to see her... and yes I read the letter later. I wanted to know what had upset her so much that she hadn't been aware of the car until it was too late."

I gasped and felt the blood draining from my head. I put my hands to my face, my elbows resting on the table. It had been my fault. How would I ever live with that. That's when I cried for the first time. The sluice gates opened and the tears poured down my cheeks. Grandad put out an unsteady hand to me, thought better of it and pulled out his soiled handkerchief. I shook my head and wiped my eyes with the napkin.

"Before the family lawyer comes this evening to read the will, I think there is something I have to tell you..." He cleared his throat, his eyes stricken.

"What is it Grandad?" I asked absently. What could he tell me that I didn't already know. It was my fault that Mom had been killed. If it hadn't been for that letter...

"It's very difficult for me to speak of this, so if you will bear with me I'll start from the beginning."

I watched him as he spoke. "Your parents met at college," he began, "and were married within the year. Your father's parents had come many years before from Germany where your grandfather had extensive business and property. He set up branches in New York. When Hitler came to power things began to get out of hand..."

'So part of me is of German stock,' I thought. Actually I wasn't too pleased about that considering I identified now with Judaism. "Go on, Grandad."

"Well he decided that he would have to go back to Germany and sell up as much as possible. You have heard of Kristalnacht: the rioting, the lootings, the rounding up of 35,000 Jews, the murders? Some of his family property was destroyed. Anyway he left with his wife against your father's advice. Your father's twin sister was due to go too, but at the last moment she developed acute appendicitis and had to be operated on. Whilst in hospital she met one of the young doctors and they fell in love. They decided to marry but thought they'd wait for the parents' return but then the war broke out and all contact was lost. Mort... your father joined the army when America went to war. He had hoped to parachute into Germany and find his parents when he discovered they had been sent to a concentration camp.

I frowned. How strange... taken with the Jews. Perhaps because of their years in America... I was also surprised to hear that my academic father had considered rescuing his parents, notwithstanding the dangers involved.

"Meanwhile your father's twin sister had married, just days before her husband was transferred to Hawaii in preparation for the war. Well, Pearl Harbour was attacked and he died with many thousands of our lads. She meanwhile was in her final months of pregnancy, and heartbroken she moved in with my daughter, your mother, and they came to stay here until the end of the war.

"In the early hours of the morning you were... I mean the baby was born, but your father's twin sister died in childbirth." Grandad stopped abruptly, his thoughts elsewhere.

"Grandad?" I prompted.

"Your mother cared for the baby from the beginning."

"Whatever happened to this cousin?" I asked surprised.

Grandad shook his head in surprise. "You still haven't made the connection, have you?"

"You mean... you were talking about me?" I was shocked. "No Grandad, you'd better explain. You were telling me about my father's background." I looked at him and suddenly something fell into place. "Grandad, are you saying that my father was Jewish?"

"No, well yes. No," he stammered.

"What do you mean, no, yes, no?"

"Your mother was Jewish, and so was your adoptive father, your uncle," he said quietly, but firmly.

My head spun. I was shocked, but still didn't quite understand. "Grandad please go on."

"The baby born in this house was you... only you were born to your father's... your adoptive father's twin sister. My daughter...

your adoptive mother couldn't have children but she loved you and cared for you from the time you were born. When your father was demobilised he was shattered to hear of his sister's death. You were formally adopted a few years after your birth."

It was too much to absorb: my parents weren't my parents but my uncle and aunt. I wasn't a Methodist, but a Jew... "What about my biological father?" I asked. "Was he Jewish?"

"No." Grandad shook his head, his eyes fierce. "His parents had been very much against the marriage. They were Southerners and I discovered that the father was a Klansman. I'm sure your father never knew, so we didn't tell them about the birth. They didn't deserve to have you."

The old man was exhausted, having to divulge a secret of such long standing was too much for him. He looked spent but watched me anxiously. I got up and went round to where he sat and put my arms around his shoulders.

"Thanks, Grandad, for telling me the truth... What I don't understand is why Mom and Dad kept it from me. I wouldn't have loved them any less."

"I don't know," he said wearily. "They begged your Grandma and myself never to talk about it, and after his parents' death in Auschwitz and his sister's – he was very close to her, your Dad – he never discussed his past again."

I needed to be alone to think. I had been left a small legacy from my biological parents which during the years had grown, and a very much larger one from Mom. In fact I had been left extremely wealthy. I guess Dad had inherited his parent's estate in New York. What, I wondered, would I need with so much money if I was going to spend the rest of my life on a kibbutz.

Grandad knew that I wanted to go back to Israel and we arranged that Mrs Forbes who'd been his cook on and off for many years and who'd just been widowed would come to live at the house and take care of him. That was a weight off my mind, as I wouldn't have left him alone and I couldn't expect him to come with me.

"Son," he said. "Will you promise me one thing?"

"Yes Grandad, what is it?"

"As soon as you and Varda are married... well, after the baby is born, will you bring them here on a visit, please?"

"Of course we'll come. Varda will love it here."

I could marry Varda as soon as I got back. I had no need to get a visa. The law of return now applied to me. I am a Jew. I was born a Jew. I savoured the sound. I wanted to stand up and shout for all to hear, but of course I didn't.

"Grandad... I had a sudden thought. I think my Dad's remains should be interred in Israel..."

He shook his head emphatically. "Your parents' remains must stay together."

"Yes of course, Grandad. Mom's remains too... I want them to have a decent burial."

"Son, your father..." The old man looked so utterly sad and shrunken, I was sorry I'd spoken. "Well he would have said something if he'd wanted his remains taken to Israel. Let them be... they've had their decent burial."

The Winds of Change

The smell of burning rubber almost choked her as she pressed her forehead against the icy window. The ground was covered in snow and the heavy, grey snow-laden clouds were ominously low in the sky. The night had passed in restless sleep punctuated by the sounds of gunfire and distant screams. Koresh... she wondered again, how will we get you released, and uncle Farhad. The call of the muezzin from the minarets sounded loud and clear: the early morning prayers, the first of the daily five prayers, the Shahada. She moved away from the window, her forehead stinging where it had been pressed against the frozen glass. She rubbed her hands trying to inject some warmth into them but it was of no use. Three weeks ago, or was it more, they had cut off the electricity, and the water supply was erratic. For a while she had used a kerosene heater but now with rationing and fuel almost impossible to get, even that was out.

She had awoken this morning in fear as she had every morning since that horrible day when they had come to take her husband. She shuddered and the tears trickled slowly down her cheeks. Koresh, his face ashen, had been polite, then angry, trying to stand up for his rights... what had he done? He wasn't guilty of anything, he paid his taxes, cared for his workers and their families, went to synagogue every Saturday and was a law-abiding citizen. They took him, protesting.

"Shahnaz," he'd managed to whisper, "The documents... burn them, all of them."

She could hear him arguing all the way down the stairs and then silence, and when she'd run in shock to the window she'd seen him bundled into a car, his face streaming with blood.

"Koresh," she'd screamed, but the car had pulled away with a screech of brakes and she'd been left trembling uncontrollably. 'Uncle Farhad... I must tell him what has happened.'

Koresh and his uncle were in partnership in the factory, Uncle Farhad and his wife Ester had taken Koresh in and with much love and pride had brought him up when his own parents had been killed in an air-crash when he was ten years old. They had two daughters, both married now and living in Israel, so Koresh was the son they had never had. The phone was silent... 'still no line,' she'd thought in desperation. 'I'll have to go over there.'

When she'd arrived at the great house, she'd parked the car in the road, and had made her way with difficulty through the snowdrifts. No one had answered her persistent knocking, so she'd gone round the back and in the kitchen she'd found Ester sitting stonefaced at the table.

"Uncle Farhad... where is he?" she'd asked urgently.

The older woman, her greying hair awry, had slowly lifted her lined face and then, rising, had taken Shahnaz into her arms, their tears intermingling. "Oh my darling," she'd sobbed, "They took him early this morning, just before dawn. I tried to warn Koresh but the lines are dead and I don't drive and the servants have gone... I'm so filled with fear..."

They had stood swaying together in their anguish.

This morning Shahnaz, her black hair neatly caught up in a band, had sponged herself down in a potful of hot water she'd boiled on a primus, taking a little for her black tea and for brushing her teeth. Now she was ready, dressed in layer upon layer, and her long shapely legs hidden in the regulation thick black stockings. She slipped on her fur jacket and then the chador, whose black shroud-like folds covered her from head to toe. She gazed at herself in disgust. How long ago was it that colour, excitement and laughter had filled the streets of Tehran. Now there were only charred shops and cinemas, smoke-filled, garbage-cluttered streets infested with rats and bodies, and milling with black-chador-garbed women; militant white-turbaned mullahs and their men, with an occasional black-turbaned, black-robed ayatolla and his followers making their way to the nearest mosque.

The weeks since Koresh and Farhad had been imprisoned had been a nightmare. Shahnaz and Ester had burned endless documents, and had stood in line for hours on end to speak with one official after another in their efforts to have their husbands released. At the factory, the workers were on strike and it was they who had accused their owners of irregularities, all unfounded. When Shahnaz had first come to the office to collect the documents from the large wall safe, a soldier had been there inspecting the telex. "What is this?" he'd growled suspiciously. "A means of contact with the Zionist dogs, no doubt." He hadn't waited for an answer from her.

They had been sent from one end of the town to another, from one government department to the next, and at the beginning Shahnaz had driven. One of the officials had come to the apartment looking for documents and, having failed to find anything, he and his men had begun to help themselves to pieces of furniture, silverware and other valuables. Shahnaz, her eyes ablaze in anger, had ordered them out.

The official, his close-set black eyes looking at her stonily had moved towards her menacingly. It was then that she'd realised just how vulnerable she was. "Excellency, my humble apologies... these things have no meaning, only my husband... I beg of you your help."

He'd seemed to relent slightly. "I must have more then..." and he waved deprecatingly at the piled-up carpets and silverware. 'Yes, yes,' she'd thought. 'A *pishkesh*, that's what he wants, but our accounts are frozen, the banks closed, wait perhaps...'

"My car, Excellency... I should like you to have it, and I know you will help..." She handed him the keys.

"I will see what can be done. I cannot promise anything," he said as he pocketed the keys.

"Your Excellency has much influence," she said persuasively, hoping it would have the desired effect, but she kept her eyes submissively turned down.

It was difficult without her car. Koresh's car had been there one day and the next had disappeared. She wasn't quite sure when that had happened. Since the street fighting, and the burning of liquor stores, boutiques and any shops carrying foreign merchandise, the buses had been running infrequently and taxis were hard to find. Shahnaz and Ester had visited their men every three weeks. Today was visiting day and Shahnaz hurried into the icy wind, grateful for her fur jacket. Only her green fear-filled eyes were visible under the chador as she made her way down the main thoroughfare towards Ester's house.

Very few of the shops were open at this hour, others just a gutted shell, and here and there bullet holes were visible where the soldiers had shot their way into the buildings. The once-clear running water in the *joub* hugging the road on either side was now sluggish brown, strewn with cartons, boxes, leaflets and sewage. The smell was nauseating and for that she was grateful for the veil over her nose. A furry animal ran between her feet and she jumped aside thinking it was a cat, but was horrified instead to see a large brown rat.

At the corner she paused uncertainly. A group of bearded men had surrounded a chadorless young woman and their taunts were clearly heard.

"Harlot... whore, infidel."

She crossed to the other side, her heart beating painfully when she remembered the same thing happening to her, and after that frightening experience she had covered herself with a chador and had never gone out without it since.

The roads were filling up. Battered cars, mudstrewn trucks and windowless buses increased in number. From a distance she could hear the cries, "*Allah u Akhbar...* God is great." Again the acrid-smelling smoke choked her and she covered her nose with her hand. The *Sepah Pass Daran*, Ayatolla Khomeini's police, were in evidence this morning and she hurried on fearfully.

She remembered the day she had become aware of the change for the first time... that late afternoon she and her mother had driven back from the henna party, the pre-marriage ceremony for brides. It seemed so long ago and yet it had been only a few months back. They'd had a wonderful day of love and laughter, when in the distance they'd seen the seething black mass.

"What could that be?" her mother had asked.

As the distance between them narrowed, they'd come face to face with a motorcycle-ridden demonstration. Thousands of black-clad men and women chanted "*La ela ha el lAlah...*" There is no God but the God in Heaven. "*Viva le Khomeini.*"

Shahnaz had pulled off the road as far as possible, and with heavily beating hearts and trembling hands they'd wound up the windows and locked the doors, hoping the crowd would pass by without incident. A knock at the window had left Shahnaz with no alternative but to open it a fraction.

"From now on all women in Iran must wear chador," the man had instructed frowning at them.

"Yes, yes," she'd said frightened. "We will." She'd wound up the window hurriedly.

They had waited for two hours for the masses to pass by, but apart from a little rocking of the car, no one interfered and it was with great relief that they were at last able to drive home. It was then they'd resolved to leave the country for a while, and Koresh and Uncle Farhad had prepared their passports, intending that the women at least should leave immediately and that they would follow in due course. Shahnaz's parents and brother had left for an extended vacation abroad, shortly after that incident. Then, before they could get away, the men had been arrested and their plans had fallen apart.

That demonstration was to be the first of a series of strikes and marches instigated initially by the leftists, amongst them the writer Rajavee who fanned the sparks of unrest delivering thousands upon thousands of leaflets denouncing Shah Mohammed Pahlavi and his Immortals, the elite guard, and all they stood for. Now these sparks had ignited there was no stopping the flames which grew higher and fanned outwards, carried by the winds of change in every direction, until the country was in revolt along its length and breadth, with street battles in every town and village; the Mujahedin and Fedayian in the north against the Tudeh, the latter, the Marxist Muslims, against the loyalists who fought for their lives and the Ayatolla and his people against all, in their desire to set up the Islamic Republic.

As Shahnaz turned into the driveway, Ester stepped out of the house, she too clad in chador.

"Good morning, darling." Her voice was muffled and she carried a basket of fruit, medicines and bread, and a new bowl for Farhad. His rice bowl had been badly chipped. This was all they were allowed to bring the men. Hot food and anything else was forbidden, and they preferred to abide by the law rather than risk further trouble for Koresh and Farhad in their already hideous existence between the walls of the prison.

On the main road they were lucky: a taxi stopped for them and within a half-hour they took their places in the already long line of women and children waiting to see their loved ones. Most of the women were silent under their chadors, their eyes downcast, some whispering amongst themselves and others keeping a watchful eye on the children. The unwashed smell that pervaded the long lines was overpowering. It seemed that many of the families had been here since before dawn. The only way to ease the pain of standing for so many hours was to squat on the ground and move half a metre or so every ten minutes.

Shahnaz wondered about these women hidden behind their veils. Many were probably wives of wealthy government officials, factory owners and others the revolutionaries had incarcerated, elevating in their stead the mullahs and pro-Ayatolla people, irrespective of their qualifications.

It was late afternoon when Shahnaz and Aunt Ester found themselves first in line. Their chadors were stained from the occasional squatting on the ground. Exhaustion etched their faces as they came face to face with Koresh and Uncle Farhad through the wire partition. The guards stood by, making it impossible to say anything of importance.

"Koresh my darling, how are you?" Her voice quavered and she was close to tears.

"Bearing up, Shahnaz, and you... how are you managing?" His chin, which last visit had been stubbled, now bore a grey-flecked dark beard, his hollowed cheeks spoke of weeks of deprivation, and his sunken eyes of untold horrors within the confines of these tightpacked walls.

"I'm doing all you asked..." she whispered. "Never a day goes by..."

"Speak up, we can't hear you." The guard glowered at her.

"The weather... is so very icy and treacherous."

She looked at his blue lips and although she had brought him a warm coat and sweaters at the last visit, he was dressed in a thin dirty brown jacket, worn at the elbows. This was not the same man who'd been taken away so many weeks ago. No, it was already almost three months.

"Koresh, we're working on it... you'll be released soon," she gulped, her eyes moist.

"*Inshallah*... I can't..."

"Time up," yelled the guard.

She stepped closer and tried to touch her husband, through the partition. "I gave my car as *pishkesh* to the official dealing with our problem, and he said soon, soon," she said softly. She turned away, as the guard shoved him roughly in the direction of the cells. 'My husband has become an emaciated old man instead of the handsome young man of only a few months ago,' she thought, her heart beating painfully against her ribcage. 'What was he about to say... I can't what? I can't take any more? Oh my poor Koresh...' They heard screams, then shots and then silence, and they looked to left and right fearfully as they made their way back to the streets, both women trembling and pale under the chador.

"Ester, how did you find Uncle Farhad in spirit?" Her glimpse of Koresh's uncle had frightened her as much as the deteriorated condition of her own husband.

"He gave me instructions... letters he wants me to write to various people he says have influence now." The older woman's voice was muffled under her chador. "You will help me Shahnaz... tonight we will write, you will stay with me... only tonight," she added when she saw the younger woman about to protest.

Both women were afraid to leave their homes unattended for fear the roaming bands of revolutionaries would take over an empty apartment. In Ester's case it was even more difficult, because the house was large and it was surprising that the officials hadn't yet appropriated it for their own needs. They each spent fearful nights alone in their own homes, counting the minutes, the hours to dawn, rigid with fear at the gunfire and shelling and screams in the dark icy night, dozing fitfully, only to waken to the terrors of reality.

As they turned into what only a few weeks ago had been Pahlavi Road but was now Enghlab... Revolution Road, they were dismayed to see people packed on balconies and walls and others massed in the roads. The women made their way carefully through the chanting crowds. "*Allah u Ahkbar,*" the men yelled in frenzy, as the mob pushed forward, and they were swept along with the tide unable to extricate themselves.

"Ester... give me your hand... Shahnaz screamed as she saw her aunt stumble. Their fingertips touched but she felt hands in the small of her back pushing her onwards, then she lost sight of Ester and the tears streamed down her cheeks. 'When will all this end?' she wondered, panic-stricken.

Ahead there seemed to be a hold-up, because the pushing crowds stopped suddenly and the frenzied cries ceased abruptly with the sound of gunfire. Shahnaz, now wild with fright, turned, as did many others trying to escape the soldiers. It was chaos as people pushed forward unafraid to die in the hope of promised Paradise, shouting "*Allah u*

Akhbar." She fought with all her strength to remain upright, knowing full well that to stumble would mean being trampled underfoot.

'Oh please God let Ester be all right... she's older, so much older and weaker than I. No, she may be twenty years older but she is a strong woman both physically and spiritually.' She searched the crowds as she ran, but knew just how futile it was. She'd never find Ester. It would be best to make her way to the house and wait there for her.

It was after six and already pitch dark when she turned wearily into the driveway, her boots sinking into deep snowdrifts. There were no lights on in the house, not even the light of flickering candles and she knew that Ester hadn't made it yet. An iciness held her heart in its frozen grip and her teeth chattered as much from fear as from the freezing conditions. She knocked on the great oak door. Surely the servant was there... Out of the corner of her eye, she saw the slightest movement of the curtain.

"Ferreshteh it's me, Shahnaz, open please. Where is my aunt?" she gasped when the door swung open.

The servant shook her head mutely, then her eyes suddenly shifty, she said "Shahnaz Khanom... Madam, *gar sabre konni ze ghoreh halva sazand.*"

If you wait the sour will become sweet... Shahnaz was astonished at Ferreshteh's words. 'Perhaps she is right. What do I do?' she wondered, panic-stricken. 'Do I call the hospitals? Do I wait? Yes I'll wait another hour or two before I start to search for Aunt Ester, she may come home unharmed. Oh please God let that be so.'

She gratefully accepted a cup of hot, black, sweetened tea from Ferreshteh, and proceeded to tell her what had happened. The woman had been with Ester's family since her youth and had followed Ester when she and Farhad had married more than thirty-five years ago. She had been devoted to the family and her care-lined face changed from concern to fear for her employer. Shahnaz looked at her, wondering whether this last remaining servant was really as loyal as Ester said.

The others had been paid off at the beginning of the troubles but seemed occasionally to reappear out of nowhere, only to disappear again with some of the household belongings.

At eight o'clock in the evening the headlights of a small car turned into the driveway and Shahnaz and Ferreshteh ran to the curtained windows, their hearts beating rapidly. A young bearded man got out and went to the other side, opening the passenger door. "God be praised," cried Shahnaz in relief, as she opened the heavy front door. Ester, her face pale, bruises and scratches on her cheeks and her arm bent close to her chest, came up the stairs, following the man.

Shahnaz looked at her in concern. "Aunt Ester are you all right? I was worried and imagined the worst possible things... I was so afraid..." She looked up expectantly at the man. He nodded reassuringly.

"Yes I'm fine..." Ester smiled bleakly. "This kind brother saved my life and I haven't thanked him properly... please come inside and join us in a hot meal. We would be most honoured, *baradar*... brother."

"Thank you *khahar*... sister," he answered abruptly, "but I must be off," and he turned to go, his shoulders hunched in his shabby overcoat.

"*Baradar*," called Shahnaz after him in thanks. "Would that Allah give you one in this world and a thousand in the next."

"All I did was for the Imam," the man answered briefly before he drove off.

"Aunt Ester, what happened to you in that crowd?"

"I was pushed along with the masses and found it almost impossible to stay upright. That man must have taken part in the demonstration, seen my predicament and rescued me, when I fell. I'm sure that he was under the impression that I was part of the demonstration. He seemed very surprised when he saw where I lived."

"I was so afraid for you Aunt Ester. What about your arm?"

"I hurt my shoulder when I fell and had he not lifted me immediately, I'd be dead by now, trampled underfoot by the masses." She shuddered.

"You should go to the *darmangah*... the hospital for treatment..."

"No, no, I will be all right," Ester smiled wryly. "The *baradar* said not to go out on the streets tonight... as if we would."

Shahnaz looked at her puzzled. "Are there more demonstrations tonight?"

"The American Embassy has been attacked, many of its citizens held hostage, and others have been evacuated."

Shahnaz's lips trembled, her hands icy cold, fear closing in on her again.

It was in the middle of Ramadan that Koresh and Farhad were released. Koresh had lost more weight and looked completely emaciated but his expressionless eyes worried Shahnaz most of all. 'Lots of sleep and good wholesome food will repair his body, but I fear for his spirit, and he tells me they did not torture him... oh how I wish it were true. I know he is trying to spare me the pain of knowing.'

In the hot shower Koresh had scrubbed, lathered and rinsed, then scrubbed again, letting the water flow over him as though to make sure he'd disposed of every last vestige of the cumulative filth of months in prison. He had been loath to turn off the water faucets. He'd slept sixteen hours, and then was ready to go back to the factory and try and salvage as much as possible of the remaining business.

The phones were again working and Ester was able to tell Koresh that Farhad had already left for the factory.

"Koresh, my son," she said. "Please be very careful, and watch Farhad for me. He is extremely angry at what the revolutionaries have done to you both, but more so because of what has happened to the factory which he has spent a lifetime developing into what it was before all this happened." She sighed worriedly. "Don't let him lose his temper... If they arrest him again, I do not believe that he would be able to cope with another incarceration."

The apartment building tenants had once been mostly Jewish, but now many Moslem families had moved in when the Jews had packed up and fled the country at the start of the unrest. Now that it was Ramadan when fasting is imperative from dawn to dusk, people ate their main meal during the very early hours before dawn. The sounds of movement began at three in the morning and the smells of cooking wafted into the bedroom and intruded upon Shahnaz's and Koresh's sleep.

It had stopped snowing although rain was expected later. The sun shone weakly for the first time in days although its rays did nothing to warm the atmosphere. Shahnaz, her chador wrapped tightly around her, made her way to *Sabzeh Maydan*, the covered bazaar downtown. She felt secure in her chador, secure from the eyes of the masses. She was anonymous, she looked like every other woman. No one was able to see her creamy skin and shiny black hair, her perfectly formed body, which once she'd been proud to display in tight, stylish trousers or light summer dresses.

The bazaar teemed with people. The high-ceilinged roof soared above the arches allowing ventilation through various skylights. The eating houses and stalls were closed because of the month's fast. She made her way through roofed alleyways passing the household wares, and the clothing lanes, the food alleys and the spice section, until she came to the alley of the silversmiths and the goldsmiths. Here were row upon row of jewellery stalls and shops.

She'd brought Koresh's Rolex for repair many months ago, but with his imprisonment and having to run around in circles trying to get him released, it had slipped her mind, until this morning, when her husband had asked what had happened to his watch. She looked at the card again, and then counted the shops. This should be the place, she thought puzzled. It seemed empty of people and in darkness. She could make out the end part of a name ...ior... the rest had been scratched out. This had to be it, Shachrior... but why was it closed?

She went up the steps into the shop nearby. "Why are they closed next door, Excellency?"

The bearded man looked worried for a moment. "What do you have with...?" he nodded his head in the direction of the closed shop.

"My husband's watch is with him..."

"Ah," he sighed, stroking his grey flecked beard, then he whispered. "SAVAK Intelligence... or rather SAVAMA now, came to take him away many months ago and he..."

"He's imprisoned?" she asked in dismay.

He shook his head slowly, looking furtively at a customer who was engrossed in the gold chains, and then whispered, "He was executed."

"Oh no... what about his brothers, his wife and family?"

He shrugged and then when the customer at last left, he straightened and said in a normal voice. "Rest of the family have fled but we do not know where. People... soldiers and police and others... have come many times to look for them. For us here it is not good but, *Inshallah...*" He shook his head fearfully. "Better you do not query anyone else."

"No... no," her lips were dry. "I won't, thank you..."

The muezzin call interrupted any more conversation and the man took up his prayer rug and, nodding briefly, left in the direction of the Mosque in the middle of the square. Men flocked towards the fountain nearby as needles to a magnet, and began to take *vouzou*, the washing of hands, drawing a water line from mid scalp to the forehead and another water line between the toes... along the foot, before entering the beautiful interior of the mosque.

Shahnaz hurried out of the bazaar. 'Koresh will be upset about his watch. No, after what he has been through, material losses of such a nature are nothing, nothing,' she mused.

The building elevator had been out of order for months now, and Shahnaz had become used to climbing three flights of stairs every day. Today she was tired, her arms ached from the heavy shopping bag she carried. She had used up all her ration coupons, standing hours in lines for the basic essentials, such as eggs and bread, and had had to pay black market prices for some of the products. Koresh deserved the best after what he'd been through and she had been cooking a great deal of the *khorishts* that he so loved. Sometimes she was lucky to get chicken, so she'd make chicken *khorisht* and when there was lamb, no matter how tough the meat might be, it was a celebration, otherwise it was *khoresht gharmeh sabzi*: a spicy vegetable stew. Koresh, when he'd been released, had had an insatiable appetite for onions and other vegetables.

Koresh was home when she opened the door. He was pale and agitated. "There is nothing left for us: the factory is being run by the mullah's men and we are not welcome there. Uncle Farhad has been all day with the lawyers, but nothing seems to be functioning and some of the remaining employees have called us Zionist dogs. Where did we go wrong? Shahnaz, we were always good to them, and I thought they would remain loyal to us, but no." He was shouting now as he paced backwards and forwards.

"Koresh, lower your voice or we'll have the police here again," she said worriedly. "It is time to cut our losses and get out of the country, you, me, uncle Farhad and Ester... the rest of the family are out and many of our friends have gone."

He shook his head. "No, we have too much to lose. We will wait until it is possible to sell, when things settle down again. This situation can't go on much longer. The Ayatolla is asking for a return to production, for a return to normal."

The phone rang shrilly and Koresh picked it up. "Ester, what has happened? Lower your voice, I can't hear you. Oh God no, when?" He replaced the receiver slowly, his hands trembling.

"What... what? Tell me, Koresh, quickly," Shahnaz cried in fear.

"Uncle Farhad has been rearrested."

"Then you must leave immediately. I have the name of someone who has been smuggling people out of the country... please Koresh. I'll stay with Ester until Uncle Farhad is released and we'll follow you."

"No, I can't leave now. There is too much to do and we have to get Farhad released. I'll return later. Please stay here until I get back," he ordered, closing the door behind him.

She sat down heavily on the carpet, her head in her hands, listening to his receding footsteps; when they had died away she allowed the tears to flow. 'Koresh must leave before it's too late. There is nothing he can do for Uncle Farhad that Ester and I can't do... he must go before it's too late.' She looked around distractedly.

Koresh's efforts were to no avail. Farhad had given him endless instructions: even sending the visitors of other prisoners to them, with instructions, whom to write to, with whom at the Ministry to talk...

It was now Friday night and Shahnaz recited the blessing as she lit the Sabbath candles. Koresh had gone to fetch Aunt Ester who had needed a lot of persuading to leave the great house, even for a few hours. She looked as though she'd aged ten years in the last few days and her walk seemed unsteady. As they sat down to the evening meal, Ester turned gravely towards Koresh.

"I fear for you too, son," she said slowly. "Shahnaz and I are as capable as you are of doing everything possible to attain a release for your uncle. You, Koresh, must leave as soon as possible, before they come to arrest you again... I could not bear it if you were to be taken away too."

"No, Aunt Ester..." Koresh looked at her stubbornly. "I could not possibly leave whilst uncle Farhad is incarcerated. It would be cowardly. I will not leave you and Shahnaz alone either, certainly not with the situation as it is here now." He leaned over and patted her hand.

On Saturday morning they went to synagogue. They hadn't attended services since Koresh's arrest, but they had a need to meet some of the congregation, to hear what had been happening with the others, who had left, who had remained, confident that the future would be good, that this was a passing phase, that everything would go back to normal, even without the Shah. People were subdued and the men, their prayer shawls around their shoulders, faced the ark murmuring the prayers.

The chadored women sat way back, most in silence, except for whispered exchanges now and again. The atmosphere was so different from the once carefree buzz of conversation mixed with prayer. Not so long ago the congregants had prayed for the Shah and his family... no longer. Shahnaz recalled how at the cinemas they'd sung the anthem while watching the enlarged portrait of the Shah on the screen, always before the start of the program. Now there were no screens, no movies: the cinemas were gutted and the Shah was ill and in exile. In such a short time their whole world had been turned upside-down.

Uncle Farhad wrote letters from prison. How he got them out was anyone's guess. Koresh went from one official to another. Ester wrote letters... All to no avail. Koresh no longer went to the factory. He moped at home when he wasn't frantically trying to release his uncle. The radio was on from morning to night and he listened in trepidation for announcements of executions and the imprisonment of well known officials of the previous regime. Never a day went by without a list of the people executed.

Three weeks after Farhad's second arrest they were horrified to hear the announcement that the enemies of the Islamic Republic had been executed and the voice on the radio proceeded to call the list of names. "Hussain Abdullah, Muhammed Bakrior, Mahmoud Mahmoudy, Ramatollah Yashar and Farhad Yom Tov..."

Tears streamed down Koresh's ashen cheeks. "Shahnaz," he cried hoarsely. "I must go... I've arranged to be smuggled out of the country... before they come for me too... I have acquired forged documents and..."

"Yes, my darling, you must go... today if possible. How?"

He picked up the phone, dialled a number and listened impatiently. "The marriage is announced," he said quaveringly. He nodded and replaced the receiver, his hands trembling. "Shahnaz, I leave in an hour. I will take the small bag with a change of clothes and shaver. I'll pay them half of what they have asked for, and when they return to Tehran with the password 'Winds of Change' you will pay them the rest. Here, put the money in a safe place."

"Of course, Koresh. I will miss you, but I am happy you are going to safety. You will join Roya and her husband Nasser in Israel?"

"Hush," he said distractedly. "Don't even mention the word. Once I arrive, you and Ester must sell the properties and come. The frozen bank accounts will eventually be released and when that happens you leave. Do you understand?" He looked at her, worried.

"Yes my love, of course I will come. First you must get out safely. Don't worry about me. I have Aunt Ester and we will look after one another."

"Come let us go to Ester's before I leave. She may not yet know about the execution."

*

Seven years without Koresh had passed strangely. Shahnaz had taken a secretarial job at what had once been the Jewish hospital. Only now it was divided into a Jewish section and a larger Moslem section. Even the kitchens had been separated, the larger going to the Moslems and the small, inadequate kitchen to the Jews.

Daily she walked through the old Jewish ghetto, past the ramshackle houses and shops on Cyrus street in the southern quarter of Tehran. She had been fearful at first but, shrouded in her chador, she was indistinguishable from the thousands of other women and she began to feel safe. She had had only one really bad experience after Koresh had left when the revolutionaries had come to arrest him.

"Where is he?" they'd demanded.

"I don't know. We are divorced. I hate him and do not know where he is now, nor do I wish to know."

They had seemed to accept that, but she had shrivelled inside. 'Please forgive me Koresh... I will always love you.'

She never went to synagogue again. Her life had revolved around Aunt Ester, whose home was eventually appropriated by the officials, but she'd been given a small room in the house, and her neighbours in the other rooms were revolutionaries and their families. After Farhad's death, Ester never really recovered from the shock. Month after month, year after year, Shahnaz would say, "Aunt Ester, let us go..." but the older woman had refused. Her daughters and Koresh had phoned periodically via France but it was only six months ago that she'd at last agreed to leave. It had taken all that time to arrange a flight to Turkey.

There was nothing left for them here. The war had taken its toll and the Iraqi air raids on Tehran had been frightening. Young boys had died for the glory of Allah with one thought only: going to Paradise. Families were forbidden to mourn, rather they were congratulated at the funerals, and were expected to be happy for their dear departed.

When the two women had finally landed in Turkey, they had been met at the airport by an old family friend, Niloefa. After the excitement, the hugs, the kisses, Niloefa, now Naomi, had insisted they discard their chadors. "If you arrive like that at Ben Gurion airport you will be mistaken for terrorists."

It had been difficult and strange at first without the chador, but both women had insisted on remaining with a black headscarf and the thick black stockings.

The arrival at Ben Gurion airport had been bewildering. Crowds of denim-clad and mini-skirted tourists and Israelis had pushed and shoved. Black-coated and fur-hatted *hassidim* had danced together in celebration... of what Shahnaz didn't know, until she'd heard an excited couple talking about the great Rabbi having arrived from Brooklyn. The crowds waiting outside for their loved ones had frightened her at first, but when she saw the joy of reunions, she realised that they were not about to be lynched.

Koresh had suddenly appeared and embraced the two women, an arm round each, and then Aunt Ester's daughters and the children were there and it had been a joyous round of news to catch up on: seven years of separation had taken its toll and in Ester's case it had been longer since the girls had left Iran and married.

When Shahnaz and Koresh had at last found themselves alone, she had looked up at a stranger. He no longer had the grey-flecked beard, and his face was clean shaven. His black chest hair showed through a brightly coloured open necked sports shirt. His eyes were alive and happy and he searched hers for the Shahnaz he had once known... His heart went out to his bewildered wife. She had finally agreed to remove the black headscarf and the heavy stockings, but with much reluctance and only after hours of persuasion. They had then spent weeks getting to know one another again. Koresh had been very patient and she was grateful.

It had taken time to get used to the dizzying noise and colour of Tel-Aviv. She remembered dimly that Tehran too had once been a happy place, perhaps not as modern as this metropolis with its traffic-congested streets, blaring radios on buses, sherut taxis, modern esplanades and bikini-clad women on the crowded beaches, the advertisements with half-naked models at the bus shelters, invariably damaged or burnt by the minority religious elements. The women were beautiful, the men handsome and confident. She had been worried by the soldiers at first but when she'd realised that they were the brothers, sons and husbands of practically every citizen, she had overcome her fear, though it had taken her time to get used to the short skirts the girl soldiers wore.

Koresh had bought an apartment in the northern suburb of Tel-Aviv. Although it was smaller than the apartment in Tehran, it was modern and airier, with all the modern conveniences one could desire. He had gone into the import business with Ester's son-in-law.

Shahnaz had arrived in a heatwave and, when there seemed no respite, she had eventually agreed to shop for light summer dresses but always wore sleeves to her elbows and skirts to mid-calf. Now she looked rather like the religious women of Bnei Braq or Mea Shearim in Jerusalem.

Friday night was family night and Shahnaz and Koresh joined Aunt Ester and her daughters for the Sabbath meal. They all lived in Ramat Gan, a separate town but an extension of Tel-Aviv so that it was difficult to know where Tel-Aviv ended and Ramat Gan began. Ester seemed to have settled down quickly surrounded by her grandchildren. The older ones spoke Farsi and were teaching her Hebrew.

"Shahnaz, you must go to Hebrew Ulpan and learn the language," said Roya, Ester's eldest daughter. "If you want to integrate quickly and feel Israeli..."

"Shahnaz gets by with English..." interposed Koresh.

"No, Roya you are right, I think I'm ready now to learn. It has taken me all these weeks to acclimatise. It isn't easy to get over seven dark and frightening years of repression, but..."

"You've done very well..." Koresh said loyally.

Shahnaz smiled. 'How lucky I am to have Koresh,' she mused. 'I was so afraid that he might have found another woman, after all, seven long years of separation is so very difficult for anyone, but for a man...'

"Shahnaz you must change your name to a Hebrew name," Nasser, Roya's husband broke into her thoughts.

"No, that is not necessary... I have remained Koresh, you are still Nasser."

"Funny, that is what Niloefa, now Naomi, said when she met us in Turkey. No, I think I'll remain Shahnaz... It is difficult enough changing the rest of me to fit in with my new country, and anyhow the kids are calling me Shani, so I suppose that could be my Hebrew name." She laughed, her green eyes reflecting the light.

The evening passed lightheartedly until Nasser nonchalantly announced that he would be leaving on Sunday for *milu'im*, army reserve duty.

"I didn't know that you had done army service." Shahnaz looked at him quizzically.

"Yes, I was in Lebanon... I am a paratrooper," he said proudly.

"Koresh, too, has done some army service."

Shahnaz looked at her husband in shocked concern.

"I was only in Haga, the national guard... so don't look so worried. My age when I joined... I was just thirty and my profile after my imprisonment prevented my going into a combat unit... hey, Shahnaz, it's all right..." He took her hand in his, and felt her trembling.

"Nasser be careful... the war in Lebanon. We heard all about it in Tehran. There was much news we never heard, but anything to do with Israelis or Americans being killed, such as the tragedy of the marines and the blowing up of the American embassy in Beirut, why there were celebrations in all the streets of Tehran."

"I'm sure you never knew that Israel entered Lebanon in order to route out the Fatah terrorists who'd become a danger to the northern settlements."

"No of course not, it was always the Zionist dogs who invaded Lebanon and were blamed for the continuing war, and the American Infidels who came to the aid of the Zionist dogs."

"The Operation Peace for Galilee should have remained just that, but Sharon took us into Beirut and it was difficult to extricate ourselves." Nasser looked thoughtful.

"I don't agree," Koresh shook his head. "I think it was the right thing to do."

"Stop, you two, before you start another political argument," Roya laughed. "These two men have different political outlooks and when they start arguing it becomes quite heated."

Shahnaz had listened quietly to the rest of the conversation. She hadn't expected this turn of events. Both men doing reserve duty... there was so much she didn't know, so much to learn yet, so much more news to catch up on. The gap of seven long years, with the isolation and repression she'd lived through made it feel double that... in a world that raced frenziedly towards the twenty-first century, while in Iran they had retreated back to the old mores and ways of the Prophet's days. She was bewildered, knew more about the Koran than she did about the Talmud and the Torah, and anxiety gnawed at her when she realised just how little she knew of the progress in the rest of the world, and how much catching up she needed.

Koresh drove her along the coastal plain and they visited Netanya, Caesarea with its ancient harbour and Roman antiquities, Haifa with the winding roads up the Carmel mountain, the golden dome of the Baha'i temple and the beautiful Persian gardens. There was so much to see and learn, new ideas to sift through and absorb.

The babel of tongues never ceased to amaze her. One minute her ears tuned to Yiddish, and the next French, English, Romanian, Polish, Hungarian. In Nahariya she heard German: the Yekkes, she was told... They had come before the Holocaust to the Yishuv.

In a khamsin, a sweltering heatwave, they drove to Jerusalem. Shahnaz was excited. She hadn't yet seen the City, and as the flat terrain sped by them, the car strained in its upward climb on the highway through the terraced hills, dotted with pine trees and rusted halftracks, left as memorials to the fallen in the War of Independence, past Mevasseret Zion and Motza. Suddenly the pale cream-coloured, stone-faced buildings came into view on top of the hill, and she let out a sigh.

"Koresh I can't believe I'm about to see Jerusalem at last. Remember the song of the Six Day War, how we sang it together with Shuli... Jerusalem of Gold?"

Koresh nodded, his eyes on the road ahead. He winced suddenly bringing his hand to his ear.

"What is it Koresh... do you have pain?"

"It's nothing, it will pass... I've had it before."

"You should have a doctor examine you." Shahnaz looked at him in concern.

"It'll pass... The doctors have treated the problem but although it is much better than it was, it seems that every now and again I have a slight recurrence of infection."

"Tell me about it, Koresh, tell me everything, also what happened when you left me so many years ago. You must talk about it." Shahnaz watched him intently.

A closed van in the oncoming traffic lane veered towards them and Koresh, in his efforts to avoid a head-on collision, turned the wheel desperately to the right. There was a shattering of glass and metal and the car spun out of control and rolled over a couple of times before coming to rest on the opposite side of the highway. Brakes screeched as drivers tried to avoid a further collision. Then there was silence.

The sound of the wailing ambulance siren brought Shahnaz back to consciousness. She opened her eyes and was confronted with half a dozen hazily concerned faces hovering above her. "You'll be all right," said a voice.

"Don't move on your own."

"Koresh," she cried out. "Are you hurt? Where is he? My husband, is he hurt?" She raised herself onto her elbow squinting into the sun, and winced with the sudden pain in her arm.

Apart from a fractured wrist, Shahnaz hadn't been hurt. Koresh had suffered severe concussion and was hospitalised for observation.

Everyone at Hadassah, from the doctors and the nurses to the cleaners, had been caring and kind. An Iranian nurse, Rachel, had insisted that Shahnaz stay with her until Koresh was well enough to be released. She was grateful for the offer, for it would have been difficult to commute between Tel-Aviv and Jerusalem every day to be with her husband. The family drove down to see them a couple of times bringing pots of chicken *khorisht* and other delicacies.

Shahnaz was relieved to see her husband regaining strength and he became impatient to leave hospital, but the doctors insisted that he stay for further observation and tests.

"What about your earache, Koresh?"

"I still have it mildly but it'll pass and it's something I have to live with. Let me tell you how it happened..."

"Please, there is so much I don't know about you since you left Iran."

"When I left you in Tehran I was taken to a place where I was given peasant clothes and we fled through Zaridan in the North. We travelled in jeeps part of the way, then we switched to camels. It was a difficult journey from the start. We passed through forests, slept in the open under trees... one night I awoke in fright to find a goat licking my face."

Shahnaz laughed. "Lucky it was a goat, it could have been worse."

"Well," continued Koresh. "The next night was worse, it was a horror. We camped for the night near the border, and I fell into an exhausted sleep, only to be woken with the most excruciating pain in my ear. I must have screamed because the guide and the others fell on me immediately, to stop me from making a noise... we were too close to the border."

"Go on, what happened then?"

"I had been stung in the ear by a scorpion."

"Oh dear God, my poor Koresh," gasped Shahnaz, horrified.

"They dragged me across the border and we got to an encampment. I don't know who they were and I was in such a state of unrelenting pain that I didn't care. An old man stood over me with a needle while the others held me down... He started to poke around in my ear, obviously trying to extract the scorpion which seemed to have been stuck... I hate even to recall the episode. Perhaps you shouldn't hear it." He groped on the covers for his wife's hand.

She squeezed his hand gently. "You must tell me everything."

"Evidently the operation was unsuccessful, because they drove me to Kabul where a doctor tried to syringe my ear. I suppose he managed to get the remains of the scorpion out but I became feverish and we had to postpone my trip. We stayed in Kabul for a couple of weeks and then... Oh, here's Aunt Ester..."

"How are you my son?" asked his aunt.

"Raring to go, Auntie. Sit down near me and tell me all your news."

It was nearly six days after the accident, and Aunt Ester suggested that Shahnaz take a bus into town. "Go see something of Jerusalem. Koresh is on the way to recovery, and I'm here... Go on," she urged.

"Thank you, Aunt Ester. Koresh, just finish the story, please, before I go."

"Well, this fellow I was telling you about," he winked at Shahnaz, "was eventually brought to Israel and the doctors here put him on a course of antibiotics which put him back on form."

Shahnaz, her wrist still in plaster, took the bus from Ein Kerem to downtown Jerusalem. She wandered along Ben Yehuda street looking at the shop windows but nothing really attracted her. The clothes were all too brightly coloured or too immodest or too short for her taste. She sauntered into a cafe and had a toasted cheese sandwich and a coffee *hafoekh*, slang for instant coffee with milk. She thought about Koresh's unhappy experience as she drank her coffee, and she shuddered. 'Poor Koresh, what he has been through, I wouldn't wish on my worst enemy.'

Although it was hot, the humidity was so much less than Tel-Aviv's, and she felt quite comfortable in her pantyhose and long-sleeved shirtwaister. She walked further, breathing in the sights and sounds, until the traffic lessened and she found herself in a narrow street with old, stone-faced houses packed closely one against the other. Laundry flapped in her face as she made her way into a second lane. The men and boys were all black-coated and black-hatted, the women modestly attired in long, calf-length skirts, either hatted or with scarves or *sheitels* hiding their hair.

The place reminded her a little of the old Jewish ghetto in Tehran and she suddenly felt very at home in these shabby narrow lanes. Young women pushed babies in strollers. All the young toddlers, boys and girls alike, had long hair. She had heard that the boys had their first haircut at age three when their lovely curls were shaved off, leaving only the side-locks.

Bearded men passed her by, averting their gaze as they neared her. She was immediately aware of a subtle difference between herself and the passing women. Her long black hair was uncovered and she withdrew her black scarf from her bag and smoothed it over her hair, tying the ends behind her. Now she looked exactly like any of the other women. She entered a dark shop, with foodstuffs. 'This is the *makolet*, the grocery shop,' she mused, and looked around.

The shelves were laden with foodstuffs and the women were shopping for Shabbat. There were various conversations going on at the same time, mostly in Yiddish, and Shahnaz listened fascinated.

"Ah Reb Finkel has made a *shiddach* for the Bloomshtain girl... from the followers of the Belze Rebbe..." said one.

"Ah Chaya Sheindel will make a good wife," said another, nodding her bewigged head.

"Rebbetzin have you heard...?"

"*Ah sheina meideleh... sholom aleichem...* What can I do for you?"

Shahnaz was suddenly aware that the woman was addressing her. "Shalom, shalom... she smiled her most winning smile.

"You, *maideleh*, must be new in the area... From which *mishpokha*, family are you?"

"I'm afraid I speak only English."

"Your family... who are they? Your nommen... er name?" she said in broken English.

"Yom Tov..." answered Shahnaz mischievously. "Shahnaz Yom Tov."

"Yom Tov? Yom Tov... What sort of a Yiddishe name is that?"

"Daughter of Jamshid Yasharel, now living in America."

"Misnagdim or Hassidim?" The woman looked puzzled.

"Neither, I'm from Iran..."

"*Meideleh* you look just like one of ours," exclaimed the woman, interested.

Shahnaz smiled. "I'd like a soft drink please. Yes, that will do." She paid the woman and moved aside to drink out of the carton cup she had been given.

"*Meine tirer neshoomer...* My dear soul," said the woman transferring her attention to a young girl.

Some of the men hurried by either going to the Yeshivah or coming from it, their *tzitzis*, the four-cornered fringed undergarment, occasionally visible. She had heard it said that these *haredi* were anti-Zionist just as the ayatollas... 'Strange,' she mused. 'Here are these ultra-orthodox Jews who are waiting for the *Mashiach*, the messiah, to come... who speak only Yiddish, for they say that Hebrew is the holy tongue for prayer only, who do not serve in the army... who are so far removed from everything I have been brought up to believe, and yet for the first time since coming here I feel at home with these people.' She shook her head puzzled. 'Yes, I feel as though I have come home.'

I've Seen Those Eyes Before

She walked quickly, staring straight ahead. Her right hand clasped the child's firmly. The streets of the *Yiddishe gasse*, the ghetto, teemed with people, most going in the same direction. Ragged children listlessly played ball, most drained of energy through severe malnutrition. A few elderly men, shabbily dressed, stood in a circle, deep in conversation. People entered and exited the old buildings, the scratched walls of which were covered in graffiti and peeling paintwork. Mothers pushed babies in prams, others carried toddlers in their arms. Two men removed a corpse from the cobblestones in the middle of the road. They lifted what had once been an emaciated old man and without any effort added his body to others already on the cart. A weeping woman followed close behind.

Fifty thousand Jews had been allocated a few streets in the quarter and whole families were pushed in together in most claustrophobic and inhumane conditions. The soldiers, black helmeted and ramrod straight, stood at the far end of the street shouting instructions, cursing the Jews and making sure that everyone wore the compulsory yellow star.

When she passed them her pulse throbbed in her temples and she lowered her eyes, hoping not to attract any untoward attention. Before leaving the building, she'd slipped into an old and faded cotton dress which hid the lines of her slim body, and she'd covered her thick chestnut hair with a kerchief.

They were nearing the central depot where the Jews had been ordered to hand in their gold and their jewellery, and she hurried, her eyes on the ever lengthening queues. Her heart beat painfully and she put a hand to her chest. What will become of Tauby if my heart gives up now, she wondered, gasping breathlessly. The hurried pace was too much for her already damaged heart. I must live to make sure no harm comes to her. She joined one of the long lines and within seconds hundreds of Jews stood behind her.

"Mama, why are we standing here?" asked the child, her blonde hair and large blue eyes giving her an angelic look, although her face and body were painfully thin.

"Hush Tauby," the woman said quietly. "We have been ordered to hand in our valuables."

"What valuables? Mama I'm tired, I don't want to stand here," the child said fretfully.

The smell of the great fire still lingered in the air. Little more than a few weeks had passed since Germany had invaded Russia and the latter before departing had set fire to many buildings in the centre of town.

"Feigie, Feigie," called someone behind her.

She turned to look over her shoulder. "Aunt Tilde, it's you. Thank God." Pulling the child along she moved back a few places to be with Tilde.

"How is the little one?" the older woman asked, her grey hair awry, her myopic eyes behind thick lenses.

"Mama, I'm hungry," whimpered Tauby.

"Hush child," said the mother.

"Here Mamaleh, I have a little bread," Aunt Tilde withdrew a brown paper wrapped parcel and broke off a small piece for the child, replacing the rest carefully in her worn leather bag.

Feigie looked around nervously. Many hungry eyes watched longingly as the bread disappeared but no one said anything. They were nearing the head of the line, where there seemed to be a commotion. An old hassid fell to the ground, his beard caked in blood. He spat out a few teeth.

Heavy black Gestapo boots kicked him savagely as he tried to protect his head with his hands. "*Shama Israel Adonai Elohainu...*" he prayed fervently. There was a cracking of bones and he lay dying in the gutter.

"That was Rabbi Bercu..." gasped a woman in horror, her hand to her mouth.

"The Rabbi? Oh no..."

"It was the Rabbi who was kicked, dear Lord."

A buzz of frightened conversation passed along the line.

"Quiet. Next." yelled a German soldier harshly, and the silenced, terrified line moved up one.

Little Tauby cringed, and buried her face in her mother's skirt. Feigie stroked her hair with a shaking hand. 'When will all this end?' she wondered. Avrom had been taken by the withdrawing Soviets who had enlisted many of the young Jewish able-bodied men. She had begged him to show them his zipper-like scar down the length of his body from his chest down to his groin, but he'd refused. 'He really thinks he can do something for the war effort,' she mused bitterly, feeling very alone and vulnerable.

"I don't know who is worse," whispered Aunt Tilde in Feigie's ear. "The Russians, in whom we pinned such high hopes in the old days, or the Germans... both anti-Semitic. Phooey."

"Shhhhh, Aunt, someone will hear you," the younger woman warned fearfully.

They handed in what little they could get away with. Both women had hidden a few gold rings and a couple of diamonds in the seams of their clothing. All Jewish assets had been confiscated by the representatives of the National Rumanian Bank when the Germans had entered the city, and the latter, together with Rumanian soldiers and local citizens, had looted Jewish homes, assaulting the owners, murdering where there was resistance and raping the women. Feigie's neighbour, Natasha, had been raped and murdered, whilst she herself had been at her brother's apartment together with the child.

Thousands of Jews had fled the town in wagons, carts and by foot in the direction of Bucharest. Whoever could get out did so. The way was perilous because of the border guards between each town. These soldiers checked the papers and belongings of the refugees and most were sent back unless they had money to buy their way through but even that didn't always work.

Feigie's brothers and their families had managed so far to stay out of the ghetto and they supported their sister and her child as best they could. However, when they too decided to flee, the problem was what do to with the two. Feigie was an attractive thirty year old, with a serious heart ailment, and Tauby a puny, malnourished child of six. It would be unwise, to say the least, to put them through the hardship of a journey. It was finally decided to put Feigie into the Jewish Hospital where most of the patients were tubercular.

The weeks and months flew by and life in the hospital took on its own routine. The constant terror of the visiting German soldiers who arrived at the entrance in buses and then spread out over the hospital yelling and prodding the patients was proving too much for Feigie.

"Mama, Mama, they're here... the soldiers are here," screamed Tauby, climbing desperately into the bed with her mother.

Under the sheets she pressed up against her mother's body. Feigie didn't move. She had been sedated against pain and seemed to be sleeping. The heavy banging of the German boots sent shivers of terror through the child's body and she trembled in fear, her thin arms tightening around her unconscious mother.

"*Raus*... out of bed immediately," yelled a soldier to the patients.

No one moved.

"*Raus*, I said," cried the German in fury. He looked icily at the doctor and pointed to Feigie.

"What are you talking about. Don't you see you have no one to take here. This woman is close to death. A matter of days... the doctor explained patiently.

"She should die sooner..." growled the German.

It was only when the sound of the receding boots disappeared altogether, that Tauby relaxed her taut muscles and the tight hold on her mother.

"Mama, Mama, wake up please..." Tears coursed down the little girl's cheeks.

"Now then, little one," said the doctor returning. "Mama will wake up when the injection wears off. Come, I will give you something to eat."

News trickled into the hospital. Thousands of Jews were being herded into cattle trains and bolted in, only to be released days later at the end of the line, when those still alive spilled out, gasping for fresh air and water.

Aunt Tilde made infrequent visits to the hospital. She was Feigie's only family left in the city and she always brought a little food which she'd managed to forage, although when asked how she'd been lucky to find whatever she brought, she'd smile and say authoritatively, "*Es, es meine liebe kinder.*"

"Auntie, don't let them take you on the train," Feigie pleaded, holding the old woman's hand between her own bony fingers.

"Hush my Feigeleh... no one is going to take Tante Tilde anywhere. The Rosens and poor Natasha's family were taken and Doctor Yermiyahu and some of the Rabbis carrying Torah books in their arms... They were surrounded by the Hassidim, otherwise the Germans would have seen the books and burnt them. They say they are taking them to Siberia."

"Siberia? Do you believe it, Auntie?" Feigie lay back weakly on her pillow.

Aunt Tilde shook her head sorrowfully but didn't say anything. They sat in silence for some time, then Tilde sighed. "It will be dark soon and the curfew will begin. I must leave now."

"When will you come again, Auntie?" asked little Tauby.

"Soon, my child, but I cannot say when." She bent down to hug the emaciated little body. "Take care of your mother, little one."

It was difficult to gauge the length of time they stayed at the hospital. It felt like a lifetime. Tauby found companions, only to lose them again and again. Either her friends died or were hauled out of bed by the Germans and sent on the transportations.

More than half of the town's Jewish population had been transported and those remaining worked at any job available, in order to avoid exile.

The law requiring Jews to wear the yellow star and the curfew were finally repealed in October 1943. Before long news filtered in that the Russians were advancing and when suddenly the Germans disappeared, the citizens went wild with joy and rushed to the gates of the city to receive their saviours with flowers and cheers.

The Russians, however, were only interested in looting. They smashed windows, broke into shops, took over houses ejecting their owners. They killed and they raped. Young women took to wearing rags, anything to make themselves unattractive to the soldiers.

"Papa, Papa..." whispered Tauby, her eyes wide in wonder. She had so often looked at the small photo Mama kept in her purse, so she was able to recognise, but only just, her father. He smiled tenderly at them and his eyes lit his gaunt, stubbled face. Feigie turned and with a cry of joy was in his arms. They embraced and Avrom drew Tauby towards him and the three held onto one another.

"I never thought I'd see either of you again," wept Avrom.

"I was afraid you'd never return..." The tears spilled from Feigie's closed eyes and rolled slowly down her pale, hollow cheeks.

They left the hospital and moved into Feigie's eldest brother's apartment, which was one of the few not yet appropriated by the Russians. Their own home had long since been taken over. Valuables had been stored before the family had fled and only the bare minimum was left.

Avrom didn't stay long. Feigie wept to see him go again, but he was young and headstrong and believed that the war would soon be over. He was still a soldier in the Red Army and was put in charge of a labour camp. When he discovered that the remaining wealthier Jews, those who owned paintings, crystal, pianos and large apartments were to be sent to Siberia, he tried to warn them. Some listened and fled, others refused to believe and fell into the trap.

Avrom's Uncle Max, who'd returned to the city, took a job as coalstoker on the train, so that they would not know that he was wealthy, but in the end he and his family were herded onto the railway platform with thousands of men, women and children. In order to stifle the screams of panic, the Russian Orchestra struck up and the trains came in and departed one after the other, transporting the remaining Jews to Siberia.

Feigie and Tauby had gone to visit Uncle Max and his family, only to hear the terrible news from the neighbours.

"Quickly Tauby, give me your hand... we must get to the station before they go... we must get them out of there." She grabbed the girl's hand firmly in her own and hurried along the streets.

"Mama you're going too quickly... I can't..."

The station was bedlam. Thousands of terrified people moved too and fro, looking for family, peering over heads, searching for their loved ones.

"Uncle Max..." cried Feigie anxiously, standing on tiptoes trying to see over the heads, but the noise was unbearable and above it all played the orchestra, the music drowning out everything else. They were pushed and she fell backwards, losing hold of the child's hand.

"Tauby...!" she screamed and with a superhuman effort she struggled to her feet and grabbed at her daughter's dress. She fought to catch her breath, and the pain in her chest was stronger than ever. "Let's get out of here, before they push us onto the train..." She had now got a firm hold on the child's hand and they elbowed their way out of the station.

The nights were becoming chilly and the days were shorter. The leaves had turned yellow, red and russet and slowly floated earthwards, leaving the trees looking bereft and bare. Feigie took painstaking trouble to make herself look as unattractive as possible. She covered her hair with a black scarf and wore a dress a few sizes too large. She made sure her legs were always clad in heavy black, woollen socks.

They made regular visits to Aunt Tilde and it was on one such visit that Feigie noticed that they had been followed.

"Tauby, don't turn your head to look," she whispered, "I think we're being followed by a Russian officer."

The girl turned her head in fright, her face paling and she pulled her mother into the doorway. "Mama I'm afraid..." Her eyes were wide in terror.

"Quiet," Feigie placed a finger on her lips. "If we don't move he'll think he's lost us."

There was a scuffling sound outside, and Tauby pulled her mother towards the stairs. "Quick Mama, I think this is Auntie Tilde's building. Let's go up..."

They took the stairs two at a time, the girl leading the way and Feigie breathlessly following. By the time her mother reached the top of the second flight and paused to catch her breath, the girl was knocking frantically on the door. There were the sounds of the safety chain being released and the key turning and Aunt Tilde opened the creaking door. She peered out in concern at the badly frightened child and then she saw Feigie gasping, her hands clasped to her chest and her face twisted in pain.

"Feigie, sit down quickly, until the pain goes."

"No, Aunt Tilde..." Tauby cried, "we're being followed. Mama must come inside..." She turned to help her mother up the last few stairs.

It was beginning to get dark when the woman felt able to move again.

"Why don't you stay the night?" begged Aunt Tilde, her worried eyes magnified behind the thick lenses. "Tauby can sleep in the big bed with me and I will make up the sofa for you."

"Thank you, Aunt, but no; we'll go back to the apartment. I feel much better now."

They donned their coats and scarves. Feigie wore an old coat of Avrom's which reached almost to the ground. She wound a woollen scarf around the child's head and they were ready to leave. Aunt Tilde watched them, troubled. "Take care Feigeleh, you don't want to have an attack again."

"Don't worry Aunt," she kissed the old woman. "It's just that I neglected to take a pill before coming, but I'm all right now and won't forget again, I promise."

When they reached the entrance, they paused in the doorway, peering stealthily out to make sure that the Russian was nowhere in sight.

"It's all right... come Tauby."

The streets were mostly deserted. There were sounds of laughter and music. The tarmac glistened when a light reflected on its wet surface, but the lights were few and far between, and soon there would be complete blackout. Feigie had hoped to reach home before it was too dark to see her way. She tried to avoid the puddles but they seemed to miss one and then slosh through the next. Their feet were cold in their wet shoes.

They paused listening. Feigie's thoughts had been fixed on getting home as soon as possible but it was the child who'd drawn her attention to the footsteps behind them. They came nearer and when they stopped the sounds stopped. Feigie peered into the darkness. She could just make out the outline of a man. Her hand which held the child's was wet with perspiration. The man, realising that they were aware of him, resumed walking and came alongside them. It was the Russian officer and he reeled slightly. He cleared his throat. "I need a place to stay," he said in guttural German; the words carried on beer-reeking breath. "I wish to stay with you in your apartment, and you will care for me."

The woman was stunned. "I... I..." she stammered. "I... I'm sorry. We have no room in the apartment."

The officer was large and stood over them menacingly. "Whatever room there is will be good enough for me. Lead the way," he commanded.

So it was that the Russian officer moved into the guest bedroom. He came home drunk most nights and she would listen in fear at the sounds of his retching. Though he never made any advances towards her, she was still fearful. He left early every morning and she would have to clear up the filthy mess, gagging as she cleaned his room. 'How much longer will this last?' she wondered again and again. Her thoughts turned to her husband. 'I haven't heard from Avroimeleh these last few months.' He had now and again managed to send word or write but for some time now there'd been silence, and she feared for him.

Months flew by, and then one night the officer came back earlier than usual and perhaps he was less drunk then he normally was, because as Feigie lay tensely listening for the sounds of vomiting which didn't come, she sat up worried, at the strange silence. There was a knock on her door.

"What is it?" she asked falteringly.

"Open, I wish to talk to you." There was a pause, then he hiccuped.

"In the morning, we will talk. The child is asleep." She pulled the covers to her chest.

He put his weight to the door and it flew open. She gaped at him in shocked surprise. "How dare you... Get out."

Tauby awoke and began to cry. Feigie took her in her arms rocking her to calm her fear, although her own heart pounded unbearably, with the sound hammering in her ears.

The Russian stared at them for some moments, his great bulk blocking the doorway. He muttered something and then backed out closing the door behind him, hiccuping as he did so. Feigie lay awake all night, fearful that he would try again to enter her room.

In the morning he was gone and she knew then that she could not spend another night under the same roof. She packed a bag with as much as she could for herself and the child and, locking the front door, she pocketed the key. Having dragged the bag down the stairs, she and Tauby stood at the kerb wondering how to get to Aunt Tilde with the heavy baggage. Traffic passed them by. She hoped a bus would stop for her even though they were some way from the nearest bus stop, the route was through their street. Motorbikes roared by, bicycle riders stared at them as they whizzed past. A rider even lifted his cap to her and she nodded. Horse-drawn wagons and carts piled high with produce clopped and creaked by on the other side of the road, and she wondered whether she could persuade one of the wagoneers to stop for her.

"Feigie," called a voice from one of the approaching wagons, and she blinked in surprise. Aunt Tilde sat up front with the driver, and they came to a screeching stop. The horses snorted and switched their tails, then the nearest horse to the kerb lifted its plaited tail and dropped a turd pat onto the tarmac.

"Aunt where are you going? We were hoping to come to you."

Aunt Tilde smiled. "I have come to collect you both. The news is that the war will end soon, and we must try to reach the rest of the family in Bucharest..." She waved a letter from her son. "Manuel has written that he has arrived in Bucharest and some of the family are there... that I should collect you and the child and take a train. The trains are full of soldiers so I thought it best... She gestured at the wagon.

The wagon driver grumbled at having to lift the heavy bag and the little girl. He was surly and bad-tempered although he had been paid well for his services. On the outskirts of town they joined the already heavy traffic in the direction of the Rumanian capital. They travelled, stopping once only by the wayside to eat. They passed tanks, the dispossessed, and stinking corpses which lay rotting and ridden with flies and maggots. They rode in silence hour after hour. The road to Roman was wide and busy. Russian soldiers marched wearily along this road and amongst them were thieves and murderers, so the wagoneer informed them. They stopped to rest in some of the small towns and travelled through the night, passing forests and unpopulated areas.

At dawn they stopped to eat some dry bread and a little ham. Having rested outside a small town, they again set out at nightfall. The road was once again filled with straggling soldiers, who called out to them, some in greeting, others cursing them, but on they rode, ignoring the stinging words.

Without any warning two grey figures sprang out of the forest, indistinct in the moonless night, and like ghosts come back from the dead they grabbed the reins, slowing down the wagon. The horses neighed in fright, both rearing on their hind legs. The wagoneer tried to calm them.

"What do you think you are doing," he cried in anger. For his pains he was hit across the head with a rifle butt, and he brought a filthy hand to his bleeding cheek. Fear shone in his eyes. Aunt Tilde grabbed the whip from him and lashed out at the men, but a hand grabbed the whip and it was pulled savagely from her hand. One of the men leaped onto the wagon and the other took the reins and walked the horses into the thick underbrush.

"Where are you taking us," cried Feigie now thoroughly frightened. "We have harmed no one, we have no valuables and hardly any food. Take what you will and let us go."

Neither man answered.

The sound of water could be heard... running water. There had to be a stream or river nearby. The branches of the trees swept against them and they ducked to avoid getting scratched. Tauby clung to her mother, too afraid to utter a word. Feigie wondered whether she should scream. No one would hear them this far from the road. 'Oh God, we've survived the war until now and are going to die in the hands of thieves.'

They came to a stop in a clearing and were told to get off the wagon. The men went through their belongings, strewing the clothes around. When they didn't find anything of value they became angry and turned on the women. There was no doubt in their minds that the two women had money or jewellery on their persons.

"Undress," ordered one of the men, looking at Feigie.

She shrank from him, and sank to her knees. "No, no we have nothing."

The child crouched with her. " Tauby," she whispered hoarsely.

"*Shreit, shreit*, scream as loudly as you can."

One of the men bent down, and pulled her up savagely by her coat lapels. She almost choked at the unwashed smell and the foul breath. The little girl let out a piercing scream, and the man let go of Feigie. His companion fired a shot into the air.

"What did you do that for, idiot?" yelled the first man, as the horses leaped forward dragging the wagon along with them, and then the wheels caught between the trees and the foliage. The wagon overturned, the reins snapped and the horses bolted. The wagoneer looked askance for a moment, decided that this was a good time to flee, turned and ran without looking backwards.

The little girl went on screaming and one of the men hit her across the head. She fell over backwards and now Feigie and Aunt Tilde joined in the screaming. The men cursed, turned tail and ran through the trees disappearing as quickly as they'd appeared on the road.

Feigie picked the child up and brushed her down. "Are you all right, my baby?" She examined the girl's head but there was no wound, only a large lump on her skull. She held her close until she stopped sobbing.

Aunt Tilde put her arms around them both. "Come," she said at last. "Let us make our way back to the road."

They sat down on a grass verge at the roadside and watched the soldiers straggling by. Blood oozed from a cut above the old lady's left eye and Feigie opened her coat and ripped the hem of her dress with her teeth. She tore off a width, and folding it in two she wound it tightly round Aunt Tilde's head, stanching the flow of blood.

A soldier came too close and Tauby screamed again. He stopped in astonishment and asked them what was wrong. He seemed very young and his blue eyes watched them curiously. His uniform was in tatters and his chin stubbled, but something about him made them realise that there was no reason to be afraid of him.

Feigie related what had happened and he nodded sympathetically. "You are Jews and I am too. My name is Vladimir Itzikovitz. Do not worry. I will see that no harm comes to you."

He arranged an escort for them and they walked beside two soldiers. The men were sympathetic and when they saw that the little girl lagged behind, one of the soldiers picked her up and carried her on his shoulders. They stopped to rest and were given a little bread and water. When at last they found a cart and horse on the road the soldiers ordered the driver to take them into the town.

*

She didn't look forward to Shabbat... Again Aunt Bella had arranged for her to visit. If only she was more like her sister, Auntie Tilde, mused the teenager. I'd much rather stay here with my friends. 'Here' was the youth village where she had her world: her education, her friends, her social and health needs. It was Youth Aliyah who cared for her needs and those of thousands of other homeless children. It was they who had brought them over in tightly packed boats at the end of the war, many of the children in advance of their parents, who would join them later.

In Tauby's case there had been no one to join her. Papa had died in the labour camp: typhoid, they had told Feigie. They had stayed in

Rumania for months and when they had at last reached Bucharest, the uncles had taken them in. Feigie had been proud and had wanted to be independent and so she'd married a middle-aged man, balding and with a paunch, and she and her daughter had gone to live in his house. Black hair grew in tufts out of his nostrils and his ears and the child had been afraid of him. He hadn't been very patient with the girl either and had done nothing to win her trust, and at last Feigie had decided that it would be best for Tauby to join Youth Aliyah, and go to Israel. She hoped to join her in a year or so, but Herman, although he had agreed initially, had no intentions whatsoever of leaving Bucharest.

The girl sighed sadly. 'If only I had my family here...' Mama had died in childbirth... She should never have gone through with it, but she'd insisted and now Tauby's half-sister was as motherless as she. Aunt Tilde too had died... she wasn't sure how, and Aunt Bella hadn't been very forthcoming. With lips set in a thin line, she had said dispassionately, "My sister Tilde died three weeks ago." She had watched Tauby weep for her aunt, but her own eyes had remained dry.

Bella was a widow and, as she had never had any children of her own, she had no idea how to deal with a teenager, especially one who'd gone through so much during the war, seen so much agony and death... a teenager who was mature beyond her years and fiercely independent.

The bus pulled in at the Egged station, and Tauby retrieved her small overnight bag from between her legs. I'll walk to Hadar, she thought. Anything to put off going to Aunt Bella's. She dawdled on the way looking into the shop windows on Rehov Herzl, then she turned up Balfour Street and climbed the steep road. Traffic was very light as people were home getting ready for the Sabbath meal. At the corner of Tel-Hai street she saw a flower stall and digging deep into her pocket she withdrew a few piastres... enough for two gladioli.

Clasping the two long stalks in one hand and the bag in the other, she turned into the pathway. Aunt Bella had a tiny two-roomed back apartment and she put down the bag to ring the doorbell, but the door opened before she could do so. "*Shalom meideleh...*" Her aunt gave the girl her cheek to be kissed. She herself had never offered to kiss her niece, never hugged her, had shown no affection whatsoever... but always proffered one of her wrinkled, leathery cheeks almost as a reluctant favour.

"Shabbat Shalom, Aunt Bella." She pushed the flowers into the woman's hand and looked around the spotless room.

"Thank you, Tauby." She added the gladioli to a vase already filled with the same flowers, and went back into the kitchen.

The table was covered in white linen and set for four people. "Are you expecting visitors for Shabbat dinner?" the girl called, interested.

"Yes, the daughter of an old schoolfriend and her son. I don't know how old he is, maybe your age, maybe younger... but be friendly, Tauby. None of your sulking, please."

"Me sulk...?" The girl looked astonished. Did Aunt Bella really think her bored silences were sulks?

"Well what would you call it?" The aunt wiped her hands on a cloth.

"Wrapped in my thoughts and dreams."

"Dreams," Aunt Bella snorted. "Leave the dreams well alone, child. Life is hard and will get harder still. Your dreams are never fulfilled, so don't waste your time. You need your wits about you for school. Finish your *bagrut*, your matriculation and then perhaps you will become a teacher, a nurse, join a kibbutz or the army, whatever."

"Those too are dreams..." protested the girl. "Aunt, I want to be a doctor, one day."

"Doctor, shmoctor..." Bella gave a mirthless laugh. "And who will pay for your extended studies? Youth Aliyah? the Agency? Who? Tell me who."

The ringing doorbell prevented any further discussion. Tauby opened the door and Bella came up behind her. The schoolfriend's daughter was an attractive fortyish and her son a good-looking boy in his twenties. Tauby's seventeen-year-old heart did a somersault and she stared open-mouthed at the youth. She felt she knew him... but where?

This Shabbat dinner was a happier one by far. Instead of the usual glum silence, the women chatted about old times and about the hardships of the present and Tauby and Zeev, for that was his name, seemed to hit it off immediately.

When the meal was at last over and the girl had washed and put away the last dish with the help of Zeev, he turned to her aunt and

with twinkling eyes asked permission to take her niece for a walk.
"We'll walk up on the Carmel, and don't worry, I will take good care
of her."

"I never worry about Tauby... she knows how to look after
herself."

They climbed the steps winding up the mountainside and arrived
breathless at the top. In Hadar it had been close and humid but here
on the mountain the cool breeze blew in from the sea and they
watched the hundreds of tiny lights in the harbour. The view from
Panorama was breathtaking. Tauby had always loved it, but tonight it
seemed special.

Zeev took her hand in his and they walked in silence, their fingers
intertwined. At last she turned to him. "You know, Zeev, I have the
queerest feeling that we have met before, but it couldn't be... you are
not in any of the Youth Aliyah villages. I don't recall meeting you
here in Haifa, so why do I feel as I do?"

He turned and they stared at one another their eyes held in a
hypnotic gaze. "Yes, I feel it too," he said softly. "It's your eyes,
Tauby. They are a beautiful blue and I've seen them somewhere...
perhaps a long time ago. Perhaps in another lifetime."

They stopped to drink *gazoz* at a kiosk and walked back to the
Panorama. Here he took her in his arms and they kissed hungrily.
Tauby had never kissed like this before and she felt her wildly beating
heart. His tongue pushed at her closed lips and when they parted, it
darted in and she felt she could swallow it whole. She let her body
melt into his and felt his hardness against her. Then she pulled back,
and his arms fell to his sides.

"No..." she whispered, her eyes shining. "Let's take it slower,
I'm a virgin..."

He looked at her in astonishment, and then with a grin, he nodded.
"I wasn't going to do anything here anyway."

Zeev had originally come to Israel with his mother at the end of
the war. He had been a seventeen-year-old soldier drafted towards the
end, into the Russian army, and as soon as they could they had
managed to get onto one of the refugee boats. Upon reaching the
shores of Palestine, the British had turned them away, and they had
waited in internment in Cyprus until finally they'd been allowed in.

"I remember the screams of the women and children on the
boat..." he said, his eyes with a faraway look, recalling other screams.

He looked suddenly at Tauby, at her blue eyes. 'I could drown myself in their depths,' he thought. 'I have seen them somewhere before.'

They planned to meet the following weekend. Suddenly Shabbat at Aunt Bella's took on a different aspect and Tauby found her thoughts in a whirl. She couldn't wait for next Shabbat and her thoughts made her blush.

Young Zeev worked on a building site with Solel Boneh during the day and at night he studied Engineering at the Technion. He had been in the army and fought in the War of Independence. Tauby worked out that he must be almost twenty-six years old... a little old for her, but she felt so comfortable with him. He kept Friday nights free for her, usually picking her up at eight in the evening after dinner and they always walked up the mountainside to sit at their favourite spot, the Panorama. Sometimes they would meet his friends and talk, but they preferred to be alone.

"What are your plans for next year?" asked Zeev. "When you finish your *bagrut* exams?"

"I'll go into the army," Tauby said with a faraway look.

"And then..." he prompted.

"I must learn a profession." 'A woman without a profession is nothing,' she mused but she didn't say so aloud.

"Yes, but what is it you want to learn?" he persisted.

"Don't laugh, Zeev... promise," she said her face flushing.

"Promise..."

"I dream of being a doctor..." She waited for him to laugh but he stared at her seriously.

"If those are your dreams then you will do it."

"Aunt Bella says it's impossible. I have no means to do so, but I shall try to get a stipend and will work and earn money."

"Perhaps you..." he stopped.

"What... Perhaps you what?" she asked.

"It's nothing. Tell me about your parents. You never mention them." Her eyes filled with tears.

"Tauby, I'm sorry. If you can't talk about them... I really shouldn't have asked. It's just that I love you and want to know everything there is to know about you."

She looked at him in happy surprise. 'He says he loves me. How long it is since I heard those precious words from Mama, and now Zeev has said them...' She dared not hope. She related what she remembered of the war. Some of the experiences were as though they had happened yesterday, other events had faded and she barely recalled them.

Shabbat flew by too quickly and she was back at the Youth Village, amongst her friends and schoolwork. The exams were fast approaching and she missed three Shabbats in a row in order to stay at the village and study. Aunt Bella who worked at the Kupat Holim Sick fund clinic went away on holiday to a Beit Havra'a, a Histadrut rest home.

Zeev phoned often, usually from a pay phone so they couldn't talk very long. Aunt Bella came back towards the end of the month and insisted that Tauby come for Shabbat. She took her books with her, but knew that with Zeev around she wouldn't be able to study.

Pesach had been late that year, and as Aunt Bella had been on holiday, she had had her Seder at the village with the other kids who had no families with whom to spend the festivals and holidays.

The Day of Independence, Yom Haatzmaut was now fast approaching and she invited Zeev to the Youth Village for the celebrations. When Thursday arrived and the last mourning note had been played for the Fallen of the War of Independence, the village lights went on and the reds, greens and yellows twinkled like a myriad of eyes.

The flags which had flown all day at half mast were now fluttering up high on the flag poles, and on all the buildings smaller flags flapped in the breeze. Accordians and guitars suddenly appeared and the crowds, including the guests, thronged to the square to join in the circles of hora dancers. Tauby and Zeev joined hands and entered the ever growing circles whirling round and round. He met her friends and teachers and they liked him; the girls especially were enchanted by his handsome looks and envied Tauby her good fortune.

"How I wish Mama had lived to see this," sighed Tauby revealing her innermost thoughts.

"Tell me how you left home after the war..." Zeev urged. "You have never spoken about that period." They were sprawled out on the grass verge, taking a rest from hours of happy dancing.

Tauby, her eyes looking into the distance, began to relate how they had travelled by wagon south in the direction of the Rumanian capital...

"Two men jumped out at us like wraiths from the dead and walked us into the forest underbrush." She was silent, recalling their terror.

Zeev, two patches of red spreading slowly up his cheeks, sat up suddenly. "Go on," he said urgently.

She talked and he listened, his excitement mounting by the minute. She was still far away in her thoughts, and she didn't notice the strange look in his eyes.

"We screamed and screamed and then this young soldier, Russian soldier, with the kindest eyes, said he too was Jewish..."

"My name is Vladimir Itzikovitz..."

"And that he would look after... What did you say?" she almost screamed at him.

"Tauby... Who would believe it. I knew I'd seen those eyes before."

"You mean you know who the soldier was... You said Vladimir, and I suddenly remembered the name after all these years. Where do you know him from?"

"My name in Russia was Vladimir, and when we arrived in Israel we changed our family name to Itzhak and Vladimir to Zeev... I was that soldier."

She took his hand in hers, the tears streaming down her cheeks. "Thank you, Vladimir, you saved our lives."

A Mother's Love

It started with a rumbling as the earth cracked. Then slowly the gap widened and there was a roar as the mud slid down the tree-lined slope, exposing the roots of the pines and leaving the wooden house perched precariously on its stilts at the edge of the chasm.

"Aaaaaaaheeeeee."

The bloodcurdling scream rent the stillness of the aftermath, and the young tea leaf pickers making their way to the fields in the early dawn shook their heads sadly. The scream had nothing to do with the landslide although it came from the exposed house.

The girl, her eyes bloodshot and her black hair awry after a restless night of tossing, turning and strange mutterings had awoken with the landslide, but she had heard only the voice inside her urging her to scream, to hit, to thrill at the sight of blood.

"Hush Lilla... Today the wise man from afar will relieve you of the evil spirit which has entered and controlled your body for so many months."

The woman, her black eyes filled with loving concern for her only daughter, bent to stroke her forehead but she withdrew her bitten hand hurriedly and stared at the teeth indentations. She sighed sadly. Her beautiful child had changed beyond recognition, from a loving, respectful girl to a wild raging animal. The hakim had been unable to help and even the Rani's personal doctor had shaken his head in puzzlement.

"Myriambai, come quickly," called her husband Mussaji.

"What is it, husband?" She stared in dismay at the fallen earth and sucked in her breath. "It is dangerous to remain in the house. What shall we do?"

"No, if we keep to the back, it will be safe and I have sent the servants to bring shovels and help and we will shore up the damage."

"In an hour, Cazi Banduji Rohekar's father-in-law from Rajpur
will be here... we must all be with Lilla. If it works we will have a
Malida thanksgiving."

Mussaji looked at his second wife in surprise. "It will happen.
The man has worked miracles and his name has preceded him here in
the north... but what do you know about conducting a Malida. Only in
the Konkan villages do we do it."

Miriambai smiled sweetly. "I know a little, only from what you
have told me and from hearsay."

The town had awoken earlier than usual to the rumbling of the
landslide and before first light the neighbours were about and the talk
was of the damage and of the coming miracle, to be performed by the
stranger with his earlocks, black beard and long white robe. Where
had he come from, this *feringhi*, they asked. From the Konkan coast,
yes, but before that? From across the Arabian sea. They nodded
satisfied.

The town, spread like wings up the foothills and overlooked by the
towering, snow-capped Himalayas, shone in the first rays of the rising
sun. Down in the valley the three-tiered red roofs of the monastery
stood out starkly against the bright light and the saffron-robed lhamas
could be seen coming and going. The air was chilly but would warm
later. Children carried books on their way to school. Women
wearing brightly coloured lunghis were already scrubbing the walls of
the rapidly growing moss, others, squatting on their haunches, broke
rocks with their hammers and chisels into minute pieces of gravel,
which would be used later for building.

In the fields young girls with heavy baskets on their backs, held
only by bands across their foreheads, were picking the tiny top leaves
which they threw into their baskets and which, when full, would be
taken for sifting, fermenting, cool wind drying, then the oven and
processing of the tea. Their young voices rose in song as they picked,
their Tibetan features engrossed in their work.

In the narrow winding lanes a cow lowered its head to nuzzle a
piece of cardboard, and as it chewed the faded lettering disappeared
bit by bit into its jaws. In the open-fronted shops the owners had
spread out the merchandise, and people were already buying
foodstuffs.

The *feringhi*, the foreigner, made his way through the winding
alleyways. Thick, tight, black curls protruded from under an

embroidered skullcap, and as he moved his earlocks swung to and fro. People turned to stare at him, as he looked so different from the other men. He stopped near the house to view the damage, shook his head, and paused at the front door to place a hand on the *mezzuzah*; then, touching his lips, he entered.

The family were already waiting in the girl's room and she snarled and screamed trying to free her hands from their bonds. He stood before the charpoy bed and watched the angry girl.

"I would like to have a full glass of water placed at the foot of the bed," he said, turning to Myriambai.

"Ram," she called the servant.

"Yes, Memsahib," he answered, entering through the door.

"Would you please bring a glass of water for the Sahib."

"When the evil spirit leaves the girl's body," the stranger continued, "it will pass through the glass which will break into many pieces. The evil one who has possessed this poor girl must not exit through the eyes or she will be blind, nor through the limbs or she will be crippled."

He clapped his hands, closed his eyes and began to pray in the ancient Hebrew tongue. The girl writhed as though in pain, thrashing and kicking and then with a final shudder she seemed to collapse within herself and the glass shattered, spilling the water and sending shards in all directions. Those present gasped at the miracle. The *feringhi* opened his eyes and smiled.

The girl sat up suddenly in confusion. "Mother, what has happened? Where am I? Why is everyone looking at me?"

There was a babel of excited voices and her mother took her in her arms and held her, their tears running rivulets down their cheeks and intermingling. Father Mussaji looked stunned and in relief turned to the miracle maker with thanks.

The servants had prepared the food and the family, friends and the stranger moved to the verandah where, squatting down, they partook of the chappattis, the curry, the green chutney pickles, dal, samosas and rice.

Lilla came through the door with her mother. She had washed and put on her best clothes. Her black hair had been braided and although she was very thin, her beauty hadn't been impaired by her unfortunate experience and she looked happy and serene. She pressed her palms together in greeting and then she moved to the farthest corner where she sat down with the women. Her proud father, brothers and male neighbours sat with the stranger.

Mussaji lifted a coconut and cracked it on the floor and then offered the contents first to the *feringhi* and then to the boys. Myriambai's Malida platter of five fruits and rice cakes, raisins, nuts, cardamom spice and rose water was laid out in thanks and in honour of the Prophet Eliyahu Hanabi whom Mussaji believed had had a hand in sending the stranger. Later the children were allowed to eat the offerings.

Much was discussed that day. Now that the evil spirit had been exorcised from Lilla's body, it was time to think of betrothal for her. Mussaji had come north many years before from the village on the Konkan coast, when he had been transferred with his regiment. There he had left his wife Sarabai and two young children with his parents, with promises to return as soon as he retired. Independence had come and the British had gone, but in the interim he had seen a beautiful local girl, had married her and although his heart lay in his village, he kept putting off the long trip back to his ancestral home and extended family.

The stranger had brought news of his family and his parents' wish to see them all again. "There is a cousin... a distant cousin of your family," explained the stranger, "who has requested me to represent him and ask for the hand of your beautiful daughter for his son Abaji of the family Nagavkar."

"Yes, yes," nodded Mussaji with satisfaction. "I know the family and if the boy wants my daughter and she him, we will bless the union. I will return to the village of my forefathers and of my parents, back to the oil presses. I shall be once more a *Shanwar Teilis*, a Saturday Sabbath observing oilman."

"Very well," said the stranger. "I will be happy to bring the good tidings to your village, and will anticipate your arrival."

There was much celebration and joy when the family finally returned to the village. They had been sad to leave Myriambai's family, their friends and neighbours up in the mountains of the north, but still the extended family was of importance to them and Mussaji hadn't meant to stay away as long as he had. They were welcomed by his ageing parents, his first wife and married children and grandchildren, uncles, aunts and cousins and the merrymaking continued for many days. Sarabai, her face lined and careworn, seemed to accept Myriambai and her children with the stoicism born of years of servitude to the menfolk.

Five women of the family, with Mussaji's old mother at the head, had decided to perform the ceremony of the serpent. They had prepared a platter of milk and rice which they brought out into the yard and, under the great banyan tree, the old woman began to chant, all the while prodding the trunk with a large stick. Lilla and her mother were close behind the women.

Slowly a large flattened head appeared from a crevice in the tree. As the body uncoiled, the head seemed to swell, and swaying slowly it moved in the direction of the chanting and prayers. Lilla held her breath... Her father had so often over the last years enthralled her with tales of her grandmother's prowess, and her faith in the powers of the Serpent God. The head moved nearer whilst the lidless eyes of the cobra remained fixed on the old woman. Slowly it moved forward and then stopped. The woman bent forward very slightly, paused and, slowly stretching out her hand above its head, her gnarled fingers released grains of *sindur* powder. The snake seemed to accept the offering and began to withdraw. Myriambai bent to place the platter at the foot of the great trunk, and the women vowed to have another ceremony at *Nag Panchami*.

Lilla, her eyes shining with excitement, turned to the other single girls who had witnessed the ceremony. "Now we will all be married soon." she said joyfully.

Preparations for the Sabbath were in full swing. The young man Abaji and his family from the next village, were expected together with the matchmaker, the *feringhi* who had worked the miracle on Lilla so many months ago, and they arrived carrying their sleeping mats. They had relatives in the village and they planned to stay with them.

All work stopped at four o'clock on Friday afternoon and even the bullocks which turned the oil presses were put out to pasture. Some of the Bnei Israel villagers had come to Mussaji in order to purchase oil for the Sabbath, both lamp oil and cooking oil. Some brought their own sesame seeds for grinding, others bought directly from the oil mill. The food for the Sabbath had been prepared and was slow cooking on a chulla stove stacked with cow dung patties. Myriambai had poured oil into a small receptacle at the bottom of the hanging lamp and she lit this, reciting the blessing.

The young people were introduced for the first time and seemed to like one another. Abaji had turned eighteen and hoped to study in Bombay. He was tall and towered above Lilla. His mother stared intently at her intended daughter-in-law, until the girl lowered her eyes in embarrassment. 'The girl is too beautiful,' she thought. 'She will not make a good wife for my only son, and what of the rumours of an evil spirit entering her. It could happen again...' She kept her fears to herself.

After Grandfather had recited *Kiddush* in Hebrew and they had all partaken of a little grape juice, the men sat down to the Sabbath meal. At last when they had finished the *puris*, the deep fried dumplings, it was the turn of the women and children. Whilst the families talked in Marathi of marriage, the young couple, having obtained permission, moved to the verandah accompanied by Lilla's youngest brother, who had strict instructions not to leave his sister alone for a moment. Sounds of sitar music wafted in from the village square accompanied by the rhythmic beat of the tabla drum.

As the weeks flew by and with the betrothal ceremony behind them, the family prepared for the wedding. They performed the Ud service held for the deceased members of the family, invoking their spiritual blessing for the actual wedding. For the seven days after Ud, five married women of the family shopped and worked long hours to prepare the wedding feasts.

The day before the wedding, Lilla took her ritual bath. She lay in the water and shivered in delight when she thought of her intended doing the same. She had fallen head over heels in love with Abaji, and she knew that he too loved her. When he looked at her with his intense black eyes, she felt she would drown in their depths. The music brought her to her feet and she dried herself hurriedly.

"Now for the *haldi*," instructed Sarabai. She turned to Myriambai and placed the bowl of turmeric mixed with coconut milk in her hands. Under the older woman's instruction, Myriambai slowly worked the paste into her daughter's skin, her face, neck and forearms, then down to her wrists and hands. She stood back to view her handiwork in satisfaction, then added a little more paste to both shoulders, rubbing gently until the skin shone.

There was happy laughter in the room next door. The five unmarried, virgin cousins who were to be bridesmaids had arrived with the bangle seller and Lilla, her face wreathed in a happy smile, entered, holding out her wrists. The dark green bangles, a symbol of fertility, were gently eased on, five on her right wrist and four on her left. Then it was the turn of the other girls and they laughed and chattered happily. When the bangle seller had been duly paid and ushered out, Lilla was fed a little rice sweetened with sugar and milk.

The laughter and music outside announced the beginning of the *Mehndi* ceremony. The bride-to-be was seated on a cot covered in garlands of flowers. Her emerald green sari with its matching head shawl seemed to accentuate her dark beauty. She smiled shyly and lowered her long black lashes.

An aunt produced the *mehndi*, the henna, and applied it to the bride's hands and feet. "Where is the special *mehndi* from Abaji?" asked one of the cousins, amidst the happy chatter.

"Here I have it... Abaji's brother brought it," said Myriambai and handed it to her sister-in-law. Lilla held out the forefinger of her left hand and the paste was smoothed on.

"Our guests have arrived," whispered one of the aunts.

Mussaji and the boys ushered in the bridegroom's representatives, his two brothers, bearing gifts for the bride from Abaji's parents.

"Lilla, open your presents," called one of her young aunts in excitement.

There were cries of approval at the platter of sweetmeats, then one by one the girl unwrapped the packages. As she withdrew brightly coloured saris and blouses, there were oohs and aahs and then as the jewellery began to emerge there were envious gasps from some of the women.

"Abaji's parents have been very generous," said Lilla quietly. She had sensed that her mother-in-law had not approved of her, but she had kept it to herself, not wishing to worry her mother. The groom's brothers then passed the gifts round for the men to see and when everyone was satisfied they made their farewells and departed politely.

Feasting began the following day at noon. The menfolk ate and made merry in a tent especially set up in the yard, and the women and children ate in the house. The same feasting took place at the home of the relatives of the bridegroom, where their friends and family came together. When the festivities were at their peak and the evening shadows lengthened it was time for the actual wedding ceremony.

Abaji began the Hebrew love song he had practised for the last few weeks and his clear voice rose through the room as Lilla entered, her long black hair loose under the sheer veil. The couple with the two fathers stood under the wedding canopy, the hupah, and the hazan began the prayers. The bridegroom lifted the goblet of grape juice to his lips and then when all had sipped of the juice wherein sparkled a pointed ring, Mussaji handed the *laccha*, a small hexagonal pendant hanging from a necklace of black and gold beads, to the groom. Abaji then carefully placed the *laccha* round his bride's neck. This she would never remove whilst her husband was alive. Abaji handed the *ketuba*, the marriage contract, to his bride and she turned.

"Father, please keep this safe for me," she said as he took the rolled document from her hands.

With the wedding celebrations at last over, Lilla took tearful farewell of her parents, brothers and the rest of the family who had gathered to see her off.

"Remember, my daughter," said Myriambai softly. "Your life is now with your husband... you belong to him, respect him and serve him well. When there is trouble between you, sort it out yourselves. Do not come to us in trouble, only in peace... remember."

With that she took leave of the girl. Abaji had hired a horsedrawn tonga and when it was piled high with the gifts from her parents and family, they climbed in themselves and the journey to her new life began.

Trouble began almost immediately upon arrival at the in-laws' home. Abaji's mother had taken her aside.

"Daughter-in-law," she said with pursed lips, "just because you have married my beloved son, does not mean that you may do as you like here. You are a stranger in this house and I am the mistress here. What I say goes... please remember that. Do you understand?" Her cold eyes scanned the girl's shocked face.

"Yes, mother-in-law," whispered Lilla, her eyes downcast. She had never been so harshly spoken to and she was in tears before the older woman had finished.

It wasn't long before both Abaji and his father began to notice the tension between the two women. Father-in-law had taken an instant liking to Lilla, as had Abaji's three unmarried sisters.

"Let me tell you a story," said Abaji's father, one evening when his wife was at the neighbours' house. "And perhaps you will understand what the meaning is of mother love and how it can be distorted because of jealousy."

The young couple sat on low wooden stools close to the old man.

"The jealousy in this case is different, but no matter," he continued. "The new bride and the mother-in-law had taken a dislike to one another, mostly from the bride's side, because she felt that her husband's mother had too much influence on him with her suffocating love." The old man paused, watching their faces, while he chewed a little pan. "You see, my children, it was like this... the young wife worked hard on her husband, who was blinded by his lust for her. Then one day she asked him if he would do whatever she asked. 'Yes, for you I will do anything,' he promised. 'Bring me your mother's heart,' she ordered. The young groom was shocked and pleaded with his bride, but she was adamant and so one night just as the monsoon was expected, he crept to his mother's house with a knife, cut out her heart and left the house hurriedly, with the dripping, bloody heart in his hands, almost demented with grief. Just then the skies opened up and it began to rain. It poured with rain and as it was dark, he could not see where he was going and so he stumbled and fell, losing the precious heart in the process. Desperately he searched on his hands and knees, and was about to give up, when he heard a tiny voice. 'Son did you hurt yourself?'"

The old man glanced at their enrapt faces. "There is nothing greater than a mother's love my dear," he said to Lilla. "You will understand it soon. Have patience and you will find that the mother of my son will love you too as she does Abaji."

"Thank you, Father-in-law," whispered Lilla, overcome.

Soon it would be time for Abaji to go to Bombay for his studies. As they could not afford for them both to go, it had been decided that Lilla would remain in the village with his parents. As the time for his departure drew nearer, the young wife sank into melancholy. She was fearful of her mother-in-law's treatment of her, now that her husband would be away, and she pleaded with Abaji. "Take me with you husband... I will work and help to support us."

"No it would be better that you stay here. Perhaps later," said Abaji regretfully.

The young bride went about her chores with a heavy heart. She no longer smiled, nor sang as she had before.

"The girl has been taken by the evil spirit once again," said Abaji's mother, matter of factly.

"No, no wife... She is sad to be left behind by her husband. We shall have to do something about it." Father-in-law, understanding the girl's fears, at last intervened and suggested that Abaji find a place of abode and he personally would bring Lilla to Bombay, and so it was agreed.

The weeks flew by without word from Abaji. Lilla worked hard cleaning, tending the chickens, grinding the wheat and corn, pounding and husking rice, cooking, carrying bucket upon bucket of water from the well. She sewed beautifully and her tiny even stitches were a joy to behold, so Mother-in-law demanded that she sew for the family and she sat hour after hour until her back ached and her eyes watered. There was so much to do that she never had a moment to herself. She was tired and wan, and had all but given up hope of joining her husband, when the letter arrived announcing that he had found them a small place in the Byculla suburb and that Lilla should join him. "You have eaten enough of my son's food," said Mother-in-law coldly, laying her hand on Lilla's belly. "Yet you have not yet produced a son."

"Yes, Mother-in-law," whispered Lilla, pale. "I will try soon."

Father-in-law was true to his word and, together with one of Abaji's sisters, they boarded the boat which carried them to the city port. The trip was slow and soon Lilla was seasick from the rolling motion. They arrived at midday to the hustle and bustle of the city.

Lilla had never been to Bombay and she was overcome with the vastness of the city and the thronging masses of people. They came from all over India: Sikhs from Amritsar, Hindus from Benares and the untouchables; many dwelled in makeshift cardboard shacks, or squatted alongside the roads.

They walked along the seafront. Beggars were everywhere. A young boy with elephantiasis, balloon-like legs and rubbery, swollen feet stretched out his hand to them, his eyes appealing.

"Babu a little something. I am hungry."

Father-in-law withdrew a coin, and suddenly they were surrounded by beggars.

Three badly disabled men, brothers, it seemed, as they all looked alike with their odd shaped heads and drooling mouths, sat in the dirt with outstretched hands. Lilla was horrified. She had never been exposed to such sights before. They walked on and paused to watch a snake charmer entice his cobra out of the basket. A small monkey attached to a chain did its tricks, somersaulting backwards and forwards obeying the commands of its owner.

Kiosks sold fruit and drinks, vendors called their wares and people stopped to eat. A woman sat near the road, ironing on a makeshift board with a heavy charcoal iron. Barbers shaved their clients on the kerb whilst young boys polished shoes. A little further along near the Prakash teahouse, men stood in a row, their backs to the crowds, relieving themselves in the public urinals.

The smell was nauseating, the air hot and sticky and Lilla felt ill. People chewed betel and expectorated onto the road. Tongas, pedicabs, rickshaws, gharries, buses, old cars and scooters sped by emitting poisonous fumes. The noise was deafening.

The couple settled in quickly in their tiny cramped room in a large dilapidated tenement building. Lilla tried to make it as comfortable as possible with the little she had brought with her. She hung photos of the family on the peeling green walls and the Sabbath lamp from the ceiling, and on the inside of the door the framed card depicting the tablets with the ten commandments. Her young husband nailed a *mezzuzah* to the doorpost, and they recited the "Shama Israel" prayer as they did every morning and every evening.

Abaji had obtained a place in the university and was registered to study accountancy in the evenings. He had found a job in the railway offices as a clerk. Lilla set out to look for work and through the wife of the *Mukkadam*, the head of the secular community, whom she'd met in the Synagogue on the first Saturday in the city, she heard that it was possible to work as a nurse's aid at one of the Bombay hospitals. As she'd had a little experience of midwifery through her mother, she applied, was accepted and told to start work the following week.

Abaji came home on Friday with two train tickets in his pocket. "I am taking you to Varanassi... it is a long journey, but it is worth seeing before we both get involved with work and my studies."

The journey was long and uncomfortable, and before long they were covered in soot from the black smoke billowing out of the steam engine's stack. They dozed at intervals, but the train was crowded and noisy so they were unable to get any real rest.

When dawn at last broke they arrived in the city, and at the banks of the Ganges, Lilla watched the crowds. Men and women washed in the murky waters. Children splashed happily. Dhows with their sails and *shikaras*, small boats, sailed by. The laundrymen, the *dhotis*, washed their heavy loads by hand, and further along the walled banks they came to the funeral pyres of burning sandalwood. The air was filled with prayers: Sanskrit chanting invoking the blessings of the various gods for the safe passage of the soul of the deceased.

An old man sat in the smouldering ashes, waiting to die, whilst his relatives stood nearby watching. Lilla stopped, "Abaji look at that poor old man... he wants to die. How sad."

They purchased banana leaf floats with little candles and flowers and gently launched them on the waters, watching whilst they bobbed to and fro and then, taking off with the current, disappeared from view, whilst Lilla and Abaji wished their silent wishes and made their silent vows. It was a very weary young couple who arrived back in Bombay late on Sunday night, and after washing and eating they both fell into an exhausted sleep.

Although they worked hard and hardly saw one another except late at night, she was away from the critical eyes of Abaji's mother and at last she felt independent and happy. She was four months pregnant before she realised the reason for her early morning sickness and her tender breasts. One of the nurses who had taken her under her wing had remarked one day that she seemed to be putting on weight. "You haven't been looking well lately, Lilla. Are you all right?"

When she heard of the early morning nausea, she burst out laughing. "You're pregnant, and you hadn't guessed it. Come, you must have an examination."

Abaji was shocked at first: how would they manage? They could barely make ends meet. The tears spilled from Lilla's eyes. "I thought you would be happy," she wept.

"Yes of course I am happy," he said guiltily, and came over to the bed putting his arms round her. "We will have a son, and he shall be called Nathu after my deceased grandfather of blessed memory."

"Yes Abaji," she answered meekly. "But why should we not have a girl?"

"A girl would be nice, but a boy must be first," her husband said firmly. "You will not be able to stay here, now that you are expecting our first child. You must go back to the village and my mother will look after you."

"No, please dear husband let me stay." She shuddered at the prospect of having to go back to her mother-in-law. "I will continue working as long as possible and will go back to my parent's village for the birth."

A boy was born at the beginning of the monsoon. The rain poured down, flooding the yard and turning it into a muddy mire. The water crept up the trunks of the coconut, peepul and banyan trees, and slowly seeped into the house. With great joy Mussaji's family prepared for the circumcision on the eighth day. Lilla did not attend but her eldest brother brought the baby into the room, set up for the ceremony. A chair with a bible on the seat was set aside for Eliyahu Hanabi, another for the *Mohel*, who performs the ceremony and a third for the *Sandak*, the godfather. On a nearby table were citrons and coconuts which were to be opened after the ceremony.

When the baby set up a lusty wailing, Lilla knew that he had entered the covenant of Abraham with the Lord, and her heart swelled with pride. Even her mother-in-law had been nice to her since the birth of little Nathu. She wondered what would have happened had she brought forth a daughter. Well, she had done things the right way round, she thought in satisfaction. 'Next time I will have a girl.'

The screeching of the cock being slaughtered out in the yard brought her out of her reverie and she peered out the window watching the servants pluck the feathers and clean the fowl. When it was cooked it was fed to the *Mohel* and immediate members of the family, although neither she nor Abaji ate. This evening we will have a *Malida*, she thought happily.

Nathu was a well-behaved baby. He cried only when hungry, so when on the twelfth day he was laid in his cradle for the first time and Abaji broke open a coconut, sprinkling the sides of the cradle with the milk, whilst reciting a prayer in Hebrew, they were surprised to hear him crying lustily. Lilla tried to calm him by singing a Marathi lullaby, but to no avail. She picked him up and rocking him in her arms she finally calmed him. "Anand is my name for you, little one. It means joy and you will always be that to us, and to your people, the Bnei Israel."

Abaji went back to Bombay, back to his studies and his work, but Lilla stayed on at her parent's home, until the fortieth day after the birth when she was due to have her purification ritual. The rain had let up, but the air was suffocatingly hot and humid, and not a breath of wind blew; the leaves in the trees rustled only when disturbed by the sudden flight of mynahs.

She was up before dawn and at first light the barber she'd summoned arrived to shave the baby's head. Catching the fine dark hairs in a starched handkerchief, she presented it to the barber, together with a coconut, rice and a few rupees. When he departed, she prepared a warm bath for herself and little Nathu. Having dressed the baby, she wound a new sari round her waist, throwing the *pallu* over her shoulder. Her mother, Myriambai, brushed her long black hair for her, threading garlands of flowers through the strands. When the *Malida* platter had been prepared and the prayers recited to the Prophet Eliyahu, the family partook of the contents.

It was on this day that the unhappy news arrived that Abaji's father had died in his sleep. The family were shocked and when Abaji arrived on the next boat from Bombay they drove in the *gharries* to the next village. Women returning from the well and carrying buckets of water on their heads acknowledged them sadly. Chickens clucked and pecked at the earth in search of food. Cows wandered along the road holding up the occasional traffic, but the drivers waited patiently for the beasts to pass before resuming the trip. The stench of the open sewers was particularly strong in the heat and humidity.

They stayed for the burial and the seven days of mourning, sitting on matting on the floor. Lilla had loved the old man and had been grateful for his understanding and patience, and she was overcome with grief.

Abaji was now head of the extended family. The house and land were his and he would have to supply dowries for his sisters' marriages which had already been arranged. His mother, knowing that she was no longer mistress of the house, had removed the *laccha* necklace which she'd worn for so many years. She became obsequious towards her daughter-in-law, but she turned her eyes away whenever the former was in her proximity.

"Mother-in-law," Lilla said quietly, a few weeks after the end of the mourning period. "Could we not be on friendlier terms? I need your wise counsel and your help and you avoid me when you possibly can... I want to be a daughter to you, not a thorn in the flesh." Her large black eyes stared imploringly at the old woman.

Slowly the woman's eyes met hers and held steady. Then she sighed. "You are right, my child. I thought you would take my son from me, but I see that is not so, instead you have borne with my jealousy and I commend you for it."

*

Abaji had completed two years of his studies and, although he'd returned to the village to take up his place as head of the family, he had not given up the idea of continuing at a later date. "Lilla," he confided. "When my sisters are married, we will sell the house and land and with my mother return to Bombay. I wish to complete my studies. You see I have become involved with a movement which is growing in the city. It concerns making *aliyah* to Israel so that we can be with our own people. At the synagogue I met with many who already have sent their children there. Many thousands of our people have already made the move and although it is said to be a hard life with much enmity from the surrounding countries, I think our place is there, for our child and for our future children." He watched his wife.

Her face had paled and her eyes were moist and sad. "Abaji, if you think that is what we should do, then I am with you, but..." she whispered in pain, "my parents and my brothers... we must take them with us."

He nodded. "Yes, I will speak with them and we will prepare to leave as soon as I have my degree, so that I will not be jobless when we arrive in our new country."

*

The persistent ringing of the doorbell was audible as the Indian music came to an end. She looked through the front door peephole before opening. An excited Abaji, or Avraham as he was now called, stood outside hopping from one foot to the next.

"What happened to your key?" she asked puzzled as she opened the door. "Why aren't you at work Abaji?"

"Lilla, my Lilla," Avraham said happily. "I came to tell you the good news... I have had a promotion and have been given the job of accountant-in-chief at the bank, the new branch, down the road, after only five years... What do you think?" His black eyes sparkled in pride in his clean shaven face.

"I am so proud of you, husband. You have worked hard, both in learning Hebrew and in taking the accountancy exams of the country."

She looked lovingly at her husband. 'He looks so young without his black beard and moustache,' she thought.

"I must go back to work. Oh yes, before I go..." He turned back, with a happy smile. "We will now be getting a telephone. The bank manager has promised."

She watched him as he hurried down the street, pausing to greet old Swartz from the *makolet*, the small grocery on the corner. How lucky she'd been to marry Abaji, she mused, and not some old man in an arranged marriage as so many of her friends had had to do. Well, hers had been arranged, she corrected herself, but she hadn't been forced to marry. She thought lovingly and sadly about her parents now long gone.

It was during the euphoria of the years after the Six Day War that finally they came to the promised land, a good few years later than they had planned. Abaji had gone on to do a higher degree, and she had given birth to three more children, had worked hard at the old hospital to help make ends meet, whilst Mother-in-law had looked after the children.

Again the doorbell rang. This time it was the new neighbour, an older woman from Morocco. "Shalom Lilla, may I come in?" She entered holding a glass in her hand. "Could I borrow some sugar, it's so hot with this *sharav*, that I can't face going out." She grimaced. "Of course, here you are Hasiba. Why don't you have a cup of tea with me?" Lillabai asked with a smile.

"Thank you, I will." The woman placed the glass of sugar on a side table and settled down on the sofa. Her eyes swept round the living room, taking in the family photos and Indian wall hangings.

"We must be one of the few Moroccans in this building," she observed. "Everyone seems to be Bnei Israel."

"We're a large extended family," laughed Lillabai. "My three brothers and their families live in the apartments, one next door, and two on the floor above us, and Abaj... I mean Avraham's mother lives with us."

"We are happy to be here in Beer Sheba, it's an improvement on our last place... but we waited many years before Shalom got a job here and we could leave Dimona," remarked Hasiba.

"Why did you go to Dimona if you didn't like it?"

"We didn't go of our own free will. In the fifties when we arrived as immigrants, we asked for a *shikun*, a small apartment in Tel-Aviv, but they said Dimona... and you know what, they took us, with our belongings, together with others in a lorry and when we saw where they were taking us, we refused to get off."

"So?" asked Lilla patiently.

"So they tipped the lorry up very slowly, until we slid off, like refuse in a dump, and it was the Ashkenasim who did it to us, the Russian and Polish bureaucrats who held the reins of government and still do," she said bitterly, accepting the strong tea with nana.

"That was most unfair," said Lilla sympathetically. " I suppose we were very lucky to come here. We had no trouble at all. Of course my husband didn't get the job he was qualified for immediately. He was a nightwatchman for a year and I worked in the supermarket, but..."

"You people had plenty of trouble before, in the early sixties, perhaps you didn't hear."

"Of course we heard, it was in all the papers in India. There we were considered Jews, and here in Israel the Rabbinate wanted to convert us, and those who wished to marry had to prove they were Jews three generations back. Then Prime Minister Levi Eshkol and his government stepped in and proclaimed us Jews, as we are and have always been."

"Say, how did Jews get to India, in the first place," asked Hasiba interested.

"The legend has it that Jews fled Upper Galilee in fear of persecution in the time of Epiphanes Antiochus, and whilst crossing the ocean, the ship sank and practically everyone drowned, except for seven men and seven women, the only survivors who were cast up on the Konkan coast, at Navgaon." Lilla paused.

"Go on," urged Hasiba.

"The bodies of those who didn't survive were mostly washed up in the same area and finally buried there, but all the belongings were lost. It is said that it was Eliyahu Hanabi who revived the unconscious survivors and that his footprints remain in a rock at the site."

"Umm," Hasiba nodded her head.

"The descendants remained for centuries completely isolated from any Jews elsewhere, and also unaware of the existence of the Cochin Jews and the Baghdadi Jews.

"It was the Baghdadis, who'd lived in India, who made trouble for the Bnei Israel here, or so I remember reading in the newspapers," said Hasiba.

"Yes," sighed Lilla. "Although we had forgotten the Hebrew language, prayers and many ceremonies, and adopted the Marathi language of the Hindus, as well as many of their customs, the Bnei Israel carried out circumcision, all the dietary laws of course, and we rested Shabbat, fasted on fast days and celebrated most of the festivals."

Abaji's mother came through the door, and the neighbour rose to greet her. "I must go, and thank you for the sugar... I will return it soon."

"Mother-in-law," said Lilla excitedly, after closing the door. She took the laden basket from the old woman. "Abaji was here to tell us his wonderful news. He has been promoted..."

The old woman straightened her sari and sat down wearily. Her ringed gnarled fingers wiped the perspiration from her brow, as she listened. She was pleased for her son, and she had always known that he would do well. For her, life in the new country had been difficult. She spoke only Marathi, had learned very little Hebrew and she was in despair over the lack of respect for the elders, and the openness and freedom of the people here.

"Here is a cup of tea for you, Mother-in-law," said the younger woman softly, placing the cup and the *idlis* rice pancakes on the table next to her. The old woman didn't open her eyes, but made a slight gesture to show she'd heard. She was fortunate, she thought, to be surrounded by her family and she occasionally met with other old folk from Bombay and Calcutta but she still felt like a stranger in a strange country. She was proud that her beloved Abaji was doing so well, but the children... Nathu, who was now Natan, would soon be in the army. He still had the grains of the conservative upbringing instilled in him, but the others were almost like the Sabras, those born here... prickly on the outside and sweet inside, like the prickly pear fruit. She shook her head sadly.

Natan finished his *bagrut*, his matriculation exams, and was inducted in August into the army. The youth and his friends were all eager to join combat units and he was placed in the tank corps and sent down to a base in the Arava for his basic training.

Lilla worried incessantly about him. Was he getting enough food?
Was he able to sleep enough hours? She knew he loved to sleep late.
On his first Shabbat home leave, she'd been shocked to see how much
weight he'd lost... the black rings under his eyes. "Don't they feed
you, Nathu?" she asked worriedly.

"Of course, Imma," he laughed tiredly. "We're in basic training,
so we don't get much sleep, but it'll get better later... don't worry,"
and he'd fallen into an exhausted sleep for twelve hours.

"Abaji, we must talk to the officers in charge: Nathu needs sleep."

"Lilla," laughed her husband. "You can't interfere with army
rules and our son would never forgive us. Don't worry, he will be all
right. I did the basic training too, even though I am now in the civil
guard, when I had *milu'im*, reserve duty."

With Natan's basic training over, he was transferred to a different
base, and seemed to enjoy army life. He continued to fall asleep as
soon as he arrived home, only to awaken late at night, when he and
his friends would meet and go out on the town.

Towards the end of his first year, he brought home a girl soldier
and introduced her to his family. Lilla had been taken aback and not a
little put out when she saw how much in love her son was... and the
girl wasn't even Bnei Israel. Sarit's great grandparents had come
from Yemen, at the turn of the century, but her grandfather had spent
some time in India, before joining the rest of the family in Israel.

Something stirred in Lilla's mind. She remembered suddenly the
matchmaker who'd brought the request for her hand from Abaji's
family, when Father had been stationed in the regiment up north.
Yes, he had come from Yemen. Something else seemed to be buried
deep in her unconscious recesses, but every time the memory began to
surface, it faded away before reaching her awareness. It was so
frustrating. 'What could it be?' she wondered.

Sarit became a fixture in the house when Nathu was home and
Lilla, after her first feelings of resentment, accepted her and grew to
love her. It was towards the end of Nathu's army service that the
young couple announced that they wanted to marry. The family were
excited and began to make plans.

"Imma, don't forget this isn't India and we needn't have more than
one wedding feast," laughed Nathu.

For Rosh Hashanna, the New Year, they had been invited to
Sarit's parents' home in a Moshav near Beer Sheba and the families

had made plans for the wedding which would be held there, under the trees near the old house. This family too was an extended one, with uncles, aunts and cousins, and after prayers and songs, they were introduced to a different fare, perhaps less spicy than their own, but just as tasty.

"My grandparents and one of my aunts and her family are missing..." said Sarit regretfully. "My grandfather has been hospitalised and they are with him."

"I hope it isn't something serious," said Lilla, looking at her.

"We hope not, although at present he's in intensive care."

They had all planned to break the Yom Kippur fast at Avraham and Lilla's place. Nathu would be away on the Golan Heights during Yom Kippur, so would not be with them.

"We will make more wedding plans without you then," Sarit laughingly told him, and they hugged one another. Lilla's mother-in-law shook her head in disapproval at the shameful display of love. It should be done in the privacy of one's own home, she thought. How things have changed.

The War broke out during the afternoon of Yom Kippur and took the country by shocked surprise. Prayers stopped immediately. Radios suddenly came to life calling soldiers to battle. Sarit disappeared and wasn't seen again for a month. Abaji was called as civil guard, to patrol the deserted streets at night. Nothing was heard from Nathu for weeks and they were sick with worry. The news was bad, the Egyptians had crossed the canal breaking through the Bar Lev line, the Syrians were advancing, and then the tide turned suddenly and there was news of Israeli victories. Hearing of so many wounded, Lilla hurried to the local hospital to offer her services and she was put to work preparing bandages and swabs.

The radio was on day and night. Names of the dead were announced. Funerals took place and the nation was stunned for weeks. Before the ceasefire was announced, there was a call from the Rambam hospital. Nathu had been seriously wounded, and the family took the long bus ride along the coast to Haifa.

Nathu's tank had been hit and he was the only one still alive, although in a coma. He had lost an eye and been slightly burned but otherwise he'd been lucky to come out of it as he had, if only he would regain consciousness... which the doctors predicted he would.

The war was now over and Nathu had been transferred at the family's request to Beer Sheba's large hospital where they would take it in turns to be with him. Sarit had returned and she and Lilla hardly ever left his bedside, endlessly talking to him, massaging his lifeless limbs, and watching as the physiotherapists moved his legs and arms, which they continued to do throughout the days.

It was in the second month that Sarit announced that her grandfather was out of hospital and feeling well enough to resume his job.

"An old man still working? What is his job," asked Lillabai surprised.

"Well," said Sarit hesitantly. "He had special powers, and he has asked to be allowed to be at Natan's bedside, so that perhaps he can help him."

"Is he a doctor?" asked Abaji.

"No... but he could easily be one," said the girl. "He discovered his powers when he was in India and worked many miracles."

"Such as?" asked Lilla hesitantly.

"I don't know the details but I know he has helped many people here in Beer Sheba and surroundings."

"All right, why not. Perhaps he can help," said Abaji.

Within hours the old man stood beside the bed. He was stooped and leaned heavily on a cane. He peered shortsightedly at Nathu and at the family and began to pray, all the while stroking the youth's forehead, above the bandaged eye. He then withdrew a little paste and rubbed, working it in with his forefinger, until the exposed part of Nathu's brow was white. He continued praying and rubbing gently for what seemed like hours, but they were surprised that only forty-five minutes had elapsed.

'He can't do anything,' thought Lilla in despair. 'No one can. My beloved son will lie like this for months maybe years...'

"Look..." Sarit's hands shook as she pointed. "Natan's eyelid flickered. I know it did. Natan, do you hear me? If you do make a sign with your eyelid."

Nothing happened, and the old man continued, then he suddenly stopped and bidding them farewell, he said hoarsely, "He will be well soon... do not worry." He disappeared without another word.

"Nathu, my beloved son," said Lilla bending over him. "Give us a sign that you can hear me."

Still nothing happened. Sarit turned to Lilla. "Perhaps you could sing the Marathi lullaby that Natan sang to me once. It is so beautiful."

Lilla began the haunting tune and while she sang she stroked Nathu's forehead working the white paste into her fingers. She sang again and again. She suddenly looked into his open eye and she stopped, her mouth wide in mid song.

"He's awake, he's awake," cried Sarit in joy.

Within a short time Nathu was released from hospital. He was fitted with a glass eye and his burns had healed leaving only very minor scarring. Although physically mended, he needed time to heal mentally. He had been through much horror.

"Grandfather would like to see you again," said Sarit one day.

"And we would like to thank him again for his help," Lilla added.

She brought the old man to see them and he was welcomed and Abaji helped to lower him into the sofa. They brought him tea and sweetmeats and couldn't thank him enough. They talked in Marathi which he had learnt in India.

"Tell us, Babu, about some of your healing in India..." said Nathu.

"Let me see... ah yes, the one I am most proud of..." He lapsed into silence as he thought. "Yes it happened up near the mountains in the North of India. The daughter of a Jewish family, a very beautiful girl, had been possessed by an evil spirit, and it was I who released her of the evil and was matchmaker too, when I helped the girl find a husband."

"Do you remember the name of the family?" asked Lilla trembling.

He thought for a while, then shook his head. "No, the father was Mussaji and the mother Myriambai, but I cannot remember the daughter's name."

Lilla fell to her knees in front of the old man. "Babu, it was me, Lilla, and I thank you for the second time." The tears streamed down her cheeks and the family looked stunned.

"No, my child..." the old man said gently. "It was mother love that helped you, your own mother who called me to your aid, and mother love that helped your son. It was you who brought him round with your Marathi lullaby, my granddaughter told me. I was only an instrument of this Mother Love."

Bewilderment

The air in the Beit Nida hut was stifling and the matting on the earth floor had turned brown with the women's perspiration. The young girl suckled her infant, her firm, brown breasts, which were swollen with milk, glistened with sweat. She looked at her companion who sat motionless near the doorway.

"At dusk I finish my forty days and will go and wash in the river... I am so happy it is over and I can be with Aklilo again."

"Vorkit, you are but a child yourself. There will be many more times you will have to isolate yourself here in the Beit Nida and when you have a daughter, it will be for eighty days. I have had seven children and have spent so much time here."

"*Ishi*, yes," sighed Vorkit. "Seven days every month with the blood, makes it much of our lives here. A woman's lot is hard."

Her companion nodded in silence, patiently waving the flies away from her lined face.

"My dream was to learn at school," continued the young girl wistfully. "Not only to read and write Amharic, as I did for four years, but to go to the big city and attain knowledge, perhaps become a teacher or a..."

"The cow you have in the sky," answered her companion compassionately, "but the milk you do not see."

Vorkit absorbed this information for a while. '*Ishi*,' she thought. 'She is right. It is of no use expecting dreams and fantasies to happen.' She stared at her neighbour with large doe-like brown eyes, under which high cheek bones accentuated a perfectly formed face.

The distant laughter of children came nearer and then two girls appeared carrying pots of food. Both children bowed in greeting, and with downcast eyes, they placed the food within the circular stone boundary outside the hut. Vorkit glanced down at the naked, sleeping infant. The crusted blood of the circumcision had now completely healed and she gently wrapped the child in a cotton cloth, laying him on the matting.

With the setting sun, the two women made their way towards the river, where they washed their clothes spreading them out on the grassy bank. Then they entered the water, washing away their last unclean signs of menstrual blood and childbirth respectively. The young girl splashed in glee enjoying the coolness of the swiftly moving waters.

When they were dressed in clean *kamises*, they made their way towards the *tukul* nearest the Nida hut. There they found the old woman awaiting them and, squatting on the matting, they had their hair plaited into tiny braids close to the scalp. Then butter was rubbed into the hair until it shone. With the task done and paid for, each woman made her separate way home.

Vorkit found the family sitting in the in-laws' *tukul* and she entered, lowering her head and eyes as she did so. She bent to kiss each member on the cheek. Aklilo's eyes had lit up in joy at the sight of his beautiful wife and young son, and he made room for them near him. *"Te'ena istelin...* how are you?" he asked.

She lowered her eyes and smiled.

The old mother had begun the *boneh* or coffee ritual, and she ground the already washed green beans with the mortar and pestle until the grains were fine, then placing a finjanlike pot, the *jevena*, on the flames, she added the coffee to the boiling water, stirring all the while.

Younger sister Uditu passed round the small white cups of *boneh* and she smiled at Vorkit as the girl stretched out both hands to accept the coffee. They drank in silence, whilst munching *kolo*, roasted chick peas. Father-in-law looked contentedly at his extended family and nodded, then he turned to his son's wife.

"Patience is bitter, but the fruits thereof are sweet."

"*Ishi* Abba," she said quietly, her eyes downcast. She waited for him to elaborate.

"Now that the young couple have a son, it is time that they have their own hut. The *tukul* has been prepared twenty strides towards the east."

"Thank you Abba," the girl said softly.

"The dowry given by your father will now be made over to you both but will always belong to you, so that if you should one day become a *galmuta*, either through divorce, desertion or death, you will have the means with which to live, you and your children."

The young couple nodded silently.

"In the herd nearby, you have a cow and two goats. With the gold in hand, do not treat it as copper," he finished.

"*Ishi, ishi*," they said in unison.

On Friday afternoon early, the men and boys finished work in the fields, and returned to their village to prepare for the Sabbath. The women and girls had been busy from early morning, cleaning, and preparing the *injirra*, sour spongy, pancake-like bread which was made from the teff grains which grew in those parts. Vorkit carefully withdrew the ready dough from the clay pot and began to knead, adding water as it was needed. The baby tied to her back murmured, but continued sleeping.

The chickens clucked and pecked at the earth looking for food. In the distance she could hear the sounds of the horn and calls of the young shepherds trying to bring in their herds and flocks before the Sabbath began. Children had been sent to the river to wash and they too laundered their clothes, the older children helping the younger. When the clothes were spread out in the grasses to dry, the children, many pot-bellied, although not through malnutrition, romped and played in the water.

Aklilo and the other men of the family had slaughtered a few chickens and, having cleaned and plucked them of their feathers, handed the fowl over to the women for cooking.

With the arrival of the Sabbath, the men and boys, washed and dressed in clean white *shamas* and wide white trousers, made their way to the small whitewashed Beit Mekdas, the synagogue which stood on the hill. The candles were already lit as they took their seats on the low wooden benches placed over straw matting. In the eastern section was the ark covered by a white cloth which contained the Orit or the Torah written in Ge'ez and in Hebrew. Only the priests were allowed in this part of the synagogue.

The elderly Kess, the priest, in his white turban and white robe, bowed to the east and prayed in Ge'ez and in Hebrew. The children then burst into song, the Hebrew words accompanied by Amharic tunes. When the service had ended, the youngsters approached the adults, taking their right hands in both their outstretched hands, and wished them Shabbat Shalom.

Later, when the men and boys returned to the *tukuls*, the villagers partook of the Sabbath bread, the *berekete*, the *injirra* and *berberi*, the hot spicy meat and lentil sauces the women had prepared, and they quenched their thirst with glasses of yellow beer-like *taleh*.

The women sat together and talked of their children, the men discussed their fields and the elders spoke of the problems of the villagers in general. The children romped and played and so the Sabbath passed more or less quietly, except for the noise of the Amharic neighbours who passed through the village on their donkeys, on their way to the Saturday market.

The peace was broken by Tariku of the neighbouring *tukul*, when he limped into the village escorted by some of his friends. His once white shirt was stained with blood and dirt and a cut under his left eye had formed a crust of coagulated blood.

"What happened, Tariku?" cried his frightened wife Lamlam, whilst some of the villagers crowded round.

"We were walking along the path when some of the villagers from the west passed by," the young man explained. "One of the men looked at me and called me 'Buda'. I will not be insulted by being likened to someone who eats the souls of humans and wears a forked and coloured tail."

"So what did you do?" asked one of the villagers.

"I answered that we are no different from them, and then they turned on me."

"We warned you not to get into fights with those people, it is dangerous for all the village..." added one of the elders.

"Abba, what would you do if you were called Buda?" asked Tariku in anguish.

"My son," answered the elder. "If a man will not learn from what he has been told, from the experiences of others, then he will learn by facing the problem on his own. I have told you many times not to react to these insults."

Vorkit was happier in her own *tukul*. The men of the family together with Aklilo had built it to withstand the elements, and the tree trunks and branches had been tied securely in a circle. Wattle and daub had been used to line the walls. The hut was topped by a thatched roof laid on horizontal beams of thick branches. Although it was without windows, there was a low door made of wood planks nailed together, whilst straw matting and goat skins covered the floor.

Preparations were in full swing for the feast. Baby Izaya had undergone his circumcision at eight days as was the custom, but the celebration was left until the mother had undergone her forty days of isolation and purification.

When the day dawned, the young mother was in a state of feverish excitement. Her parents and siblings were due to arrive from the neighbouring village and she hadn't seen them since her marriage. Vorkit had been twelve years of age when she'd married the eighteen year old Aklilo the previous year, but it had been difficult for her to be parted from her mother. She'd wept for days and the young husband had lost patience, and for a while there had been strife and sulks.

The ululating of the village women announced the arrival of the visitors and Vorkit ran to embrace her mother. She bent to kiss her father's knees and her brothers and young sisters each received hearty kisses on both cheeks. They rested in the *tukul*, whilst their daughter washed their feet in warm water, as was the custom with honoured guests who stayed overnight.

The revelry went on until late at night. A sheep had been slaughtered and the women had cooked and prepared for days. The elders sat round the fire hypnotised by the coloured flames, and waved away the flies with their white horsetail fly swatters. The young men danced to the clapping and the drums, and the young women ululated whilst the children ran to and fro in excitement. Baby Izaya slept through the commotion only to awaken in order to suckle.

"How have things been with you my daughter?" asked her mother.

"I miss you so much, all of you, and I cried for days, weeks after I arrived in this village, though Aklilo's family have been good to me, but..."

"But..." said her mother with a smile, "the bitterest seeds with mother are better than the best food in the stranger's home." Vorkit laughed and hugged her mother.

When the visitors departed, the villagers settled down to everyday activities. The women weaved baskets and containers, embroidered, cooked, prepared dough for the *injirra*, shopped and sold at the market. The men and boys ploughed and planted, sowed and harvested and in their spare time wove cotton on the looms, while the blacksmiths' hammers could be heard as they worked on the ploughs, sickles and tools. Some of the villagers modelled little clay figurines and dolls which were sold at the market. Children had a few hours of schooling each day, but most of the boys were needed in the fields and the girls were required to help their mothers with cooking, carrying water in clay jars from the river and dried twigs for the fires, and were in charge of caring for the toddlers.

Occasionally word filtered in about neighbouring Falasha villages going up in flames, men taken as slaves, women raped and children killed. The villagers lived in constant fear that they too would one day be attacked by the rebels. The Falashas, strangers, as they were called by others, lived mostly in the northwest highlands of the Gondar province, in this ancient land known in the Bible as Cush. They were a peace-loving people who referred to themselves as Beta Israel.

It was July and the *meher* rains had been expected but the skies were clear blue without a trace of clouds, and as sowing usually started at the beginning of the rainy season, the villagers began to worry. Day after day they waited for the rain but to no avail. As the hot dry weeks passed, it was evident that the country was in the grip of a drought. It was a worrying time for the elders of the village, for they knew that if the drought were to continue it would lead to famine.

For months rumours abounded about neighbouring villagers leaving for Jerusalem. One day just as dusk had fallen, a stranger arrived on horseback and was greeted by the elders. The old men in their white turbans and greying beards sat huddled together with the stranger and the rest of the villagers were left to wonder what it was all about.

When the stranger rode out of the village, the elders called a meeting. Everyone crowded round expectantly.

"The man from the city who has been conversing with us reports that there is fighting in parts of the country. It is time we of Beta Israel were amongst our own people. We do not know what will happen. Our brethren have begun to make the long journey to Jerusalem which with God's help we will all live to see."

"How is it to be done, which route is to be taken?" asked Aklilo.

"The route is westwards, towards Sudan."

"Abba," said one of the men quietly, "we must walk many long and difficult days to the border and the way is fraught with danger. There are wild animals to attack us, *shifta*, bandits and outlaws to rob us and then the rebel soldiers will shoot us if they catch us. Who can take such danger upon himself and lead his family to their deaths?"

"My son," answered another elder with quiet dignity, "when one thread joins with other threads, then it can bind a lion."

"Then we will make our way to the Sudanese border," called Aklilo's father, "but the old and the sick and the weak will wait for other ways to get to Jerusalem."

Days passed in preparation, in deliberation, in uncertainty. Families were divided, the young loath to leave their parents and grandparents and the elders just as adamant that they should go.

"Vorkit and the baby should stay then with you Abba," Aklilo said to his father, when it was discovered that the latter suffered pains in his legs and would not be able to walk the long journey.

"No, my son, she is young and healthy, and she should go with you. You will have many more children when you get to Jerusalem and with the help of heaven and the angels who care for us we will all get to make the journey some day."

The night of departure was a sad one. Twenty adults and children were to leave in the first batch. Amongst them Vorkit and the baby on her back, together with Aklilo and his brother Mamo and sister Uditu. A brother and sister stayed behind to care for their parents. Tears flowed freely as they took their leave of the village. Amidst the excitement there was sadness and fear. When would they see their loved ones again, if ever? Would they themselves survive the dangers of the long journey? And if they did what would it be like in Jerusalem? Vorkit's parents and siblings had already departed with a group from their village, leaving only her old grandparents with an uncle and his family.

One of the elders had paid the guide half of what had been asked. "Aklilo, you and Tariku are in charge. The second half of the money is to be paid when you get to the border and not before... no matter what happens."

"Yes Abba," answered the young man solemnly. "I promise. Have no fear. We will care for the women and children and will make sure nothing untoward happens."

They set off behind the guide. No one said a word and the only sounds were those of the crunching of stones under their feet and those of the donkeys. The two animals carried their foodstuffs and jerrycans of water. The baby was asleep on Vorkit's back but awoke after a few hours and wailed hungrily.

"Keep your baby quiet," said the guide roughly. "It is dangerous as there could be rebel soldiers or even outlaws waiting to shoot us."

"Then we must stop to rest and feed the little one. The children and women need to rest also," ordered Aklilo.

At daybreak they set off again. They left behind the green teff fields, the mimosa and baobab trees. Vorkit carried a large sunshade which protected her and the baby from the rising heat of the sun. Aklilo fell in step with the guide and Tariku brought up the rear. His wife complained bitterly of pains in her legs and in her back. The children were restless.

"When will we come to Sudan... I don't want to walk," cried a little girl.

"I want to ride a donkey," said another.

They stopped again to rest and to drink a little. Vorkit's back ached under the weight of the child. He was now just over a year old and quite a heavy load to carry over a distance. He was awake and restless and flailed with his arms. She unwound the shawl which tied him to her, and sat him down on the hot sand. Izaya smiled, displaying his few gleaming white front teeth.

Tariku's wife Lamlam made her way over the stones and sat down beside Vorkit. "I don't think I can walk to Sudan," she complained bitterly. "My legs hurt and I'm pregnant and..." The tears flowed down her cheeks.

"Lamlam, we must carry on," said Vorkit, concerned. "Perhaps we can ask the men to let you ride the donkey."

"*Ishi*. Yes please."

"Tariku, Aklilo," called Vorkit.

"What is it?" asked Aklilo coming alongside her. "Is the boy all right?"

"Yes, it's Lamlam..."

"That is Tariku's concern... Tariku," he called.

When they set off again Lamlam was astride the donkey, and the jerrycans were now in the hands of some of the young men. The sun was hot and burned down on them with an intensity they hadn't anticipated. It made the going slower and thirst more prevalent, but they had agreed to ration the water, and so each person was allowed only a few sips every few hours.

When night fell they ate and drank a little and huddled together to sleep. Hyenas howled and baboons chattered nearby. The guide was disgruntled at the slow pace. "It is dangerous for me, more so than for you," he told the young men. "It is best to pay me in full so that if anything happens to any of you, I will have my money."

"Then you will run away and leave us. We will pay you when you take us to the border with Sudan," answered Tariku.

They woke the children and set out again. It had been difficult to get the sleeping children to move and some clung to their parents, asking to be carried. Lamlam had again mounted the donkey, although her husband Tariku had argued that it was the turn of one of the other women who had complained of blistered feet.

Vorkit had dozed restlessly, the sleeping child pressed against her. When he had moved she'd awoken. She hadn't slept properly for the last three nights and she was exhausted. She would have liked to ride the donkey for awhile but Lamlam had appropriated it and the other donkey carried a heavy load.

They made their way up a steep hill, then down over rocks, loosening the stones which rolled down the hill and caused them to lose their footing. "Careful everyone," called Aklilo. "We can't have accidents here."

There was a sudden scream and one of the boys, having lost his footing, bounced from rock to rock coming to a stop at the bottom of the ravine. He lay still.

"My son!" screamed his mother, covering her eyes with her hands.

"Wait here, everyone," ordered the guide and he watched as the boy's father together with Aklilo and Tariku climbed down the rock face.

The boy was dead and there was nothing they could do but bury him under a pile of rocks. "My son, my child," wept his mother. She sat down and refused to move. "We will all die... I knew it. We will never get to Sudan any of us. I want to go back to the village to my parents... I won't go on."

When they finally moved again, the sun was on the wane and the shadows lengthening. They stopped to rest and drink a little. Izaya began to wail and Vorkit gave him her breast. The child pushed it away, crying fretfully.

"What is wrong with our son?" asked Aklilo sitting down beside his wife.

"I don't know, husband," she answered worriedly. "He is hot to the touch and has refused to drink all day."

"Why did you not tell me?" Aklilo looked at her in dismay. "He is sick, but we must get him to take the milk."

"I fear that my milk has dried," she said sadly, "but I have tried to give him water and he will not take it."

Aklilo poured a little water onto a cloth and wiped the child's flushed face. "Here Izaya, you must drink a little."

"I should have stayed in the village with the child," cried Vorkit, the tears spilling from her eyes. "I think that I am pregnant again and I don't want to go to Sudan, nor to Jerusalem... I want my mother."

"Your mother is on her way to Sudan, or with luck has already arrived there," retorted Aklilo angrily. "We must go on and get there as quickly as possible."

They continued until it was too dark to see their way and settled down for the night. The hyenas seemed closer and the men took turns in keeping watch. Towards dawn they woke to the sound of clattering hooves.

"*Shifta*, bandits, hide everyone, behind the rocks," yelled the guide.

The bandits had spotted one of the children and he fell to the ground as the shots rang out. His mother ran towards him with a scream and she too was shot down. The horsemen, their black and white robes and turbans flowing behind them turned.

"They're coming back," screamed Lamlam. "They'll kill us all."

"Quiet," retorted Tariku, pushing her down behind a rock. He had his hand over her mouth.

Further shots rang out but this time they seemed to be coming from the opposite direction. The bandits had heard them too and reined in their horses, once again turning and galloped into the mountains.

Army trucks roared past and the villagers stared in fear, from behind the rocks. "It's the soldiers, they'll kill us if they find us," whispered Aklilo to Vorkit.

"They seem to have passed and at least they frightened off the *shifta*, who knew we were hiding and would have finished us all off."

Tariku wiped the perspiration from his forehead, as they watched the dust settling behind the disappearing trucks.

The guide seemed to have vanished. The men searched but there was no sign of him. "He took fright and ran away," Tariku frowned angrily.

"Just as well we didn't pay him when he demanded the money... I didn't trust him from the beginning," retorted Aklilo.

"The money..." gasped Tariku, his eyes wide. "I had it tied in a bag around my waist. It's gone."

"He took it, the guide stole it while you slept, while we all slept... that's why he said it was his turn to keep watch and he could do it alone."

"My child... my child," screamed one of the women. "He's gone."

"He must be here somewhere, perhaps he wandered off to play. We'll find him," said her husband.

Some of the men went in different directions calling "Isak, Isak, where are you?" The cries echoed off the rocks. Hours were lost in searching for the child but to no avail.

"Is it possible that the guide kidnapped him?" asked Vorkit.

"But why, of what use would a four-year-old child be to the guide?" asked the unhappy father.

Lamlam and some of the other young women started wailing.

"We'll all die here," cried one.

"We'll never find our way to the border," wept another.

"Quiet everybody," ordered Aklilo sombrely. "We will continue. The border is in that direction." He pointed due west. It will take us another three days to get there. Let us move."

"No," cried the mother of the missing child. "We can't leave until we find my boy. She turned appealingly to her husband.

"We will stay and continue the search," he said firmly.

"You must move on for the sake of your two other children," argued Aklilo.

At last the couple agreed but with pain in their eyes.

"Are you all ready?" called Aklilo. "You will follow me."

"No," screamed Lamlam. "I want to go back to the village... I am pregnant and I am sick and I don't wish to go to Sudan."

"I want to go back to my parents," cried the woman whose son had fallen down the rock face.

"Izaya is very feverish... I think it would be better if I went back with him," said Vorkit quietly.

The men consulted with one another and finally it was decided that Tariku would escort his wife, Vorkit and the third woman back to the village.

"Tariku, you can come when the next group leave the village. In fact you will have to lead them," said Aklilo to his friend.

"Vorkit, kiss my parents for me and look after our child. I will try to get you to Jerusalem some other way. God be with you all."

They watched as the small group turned back with the donkey, one of the jerrycans of water and a small bundle of food. Aklilo sighed and flanked by his brother Mamo and sister Uditu, he led them westwards.

Seven days later a ragged youth arrived in the village. He limped, his bare feet blistered, his arms and legs were bloodstained and he gasped for water. At the nearest *tukul* he collapsed.

"It's Mamo... it's Mamo."

"Bring a jar of water to pour over him and another for him to drink from," ordered one of the elders.

As the water washed over him, he opened his eyes. "Vorkit, Izaya the others... where?" he gasped.

"They arrived two days ago. The baby is sick but we hope he will recover. Now tell us what happened and why you returned on your own," said one of the villagers.

The parents arrived, the father having been summoned from the fields, and the mother from the river, where she'd gone to collect water.

"Mamo, my son, what has happened?" asked his father worriedly.

"The rebels came. We tried to hide but they found some of the group. They shot Aklilo and some of the other men."

There was a painful silence whilst Mamo's parents digested the bitter news.

"The women and children?" asked one of the villagers urgently.

"Which of the men are alive?" cried a women.

"I don't know, I saw Aklilo fall and some of the others and then the rebels passed by and I whispered to Uditu that I would go back to the village and tell you what happened."

"Why didn't you bring Uditu with you?" asked his mother angrily.

"She was very weak and the women said that they were closer to Sudan than the village. Uditu cried, but she agreed to carry on."

"What about the bodies, were they buried?" asked Mamo's father, his face haggard.

"They buried them under stones, but they told me to go quickly so I don't know more than I have already told you."

Vorkit cried for days. Izaya was under the care of her mother-in-law and the fever seemed to have receded. "I am a *galmuta* now," she wept, "a woman without a man. My parents have gone. Who will care for me?"

She thought back sadly to their wedding: Aklilo in his red and white headband, handsome and young, the ceremony with the Kess and her parents, the signing of the papers, then the sounds of the shofar and the ululating of the women, when she'd arrived dressed in her new kamis and jewellery and seated on the mule... just like a queen. The elder reporting back to her parents, the ending of her virginity... how afraid she had been. My life is over, she thought, and she looked into the bleak and lonely future facing her.

The seasons came and went. Vorkit now carried her baby girl on her back and young Izaya, long recovered from his fever, romped amongst the other children. There had been no word from Uditu and the others. No one knew for sure who amongst the men had been killed, other than Aklilo, or whether the survivors had made it across the border. Were they in Jerusalem now or were they also dead? If only they could get news.

Vorkit and Tariku's wife, Lamlam, had given birth within a couple of days of one another, and together they had spent their isolation in the Beit Nida, Lamlam for the forty days for a son and Vorkit for the eighty days required for her daughter.

With those difficult days passed, Tariku had appeared one night in her *tukul*. "Vorkit... you are lonely and a *galmuta*. It is not good to be without a man. Aklilo was my friend and I wish to be with you, and to protect you."

Vorkit's heart leapt... Why, she'd never thought of Tariku as her mate. Yes she had, she grudgingly admitted to herself, but because Lamlam was her friend, she had never dared to consider it.

"What will Lamlam say?" Vorkit asked softly, her eyes downcast.

"Lamlam will have to agree... I have decided and if you will have me, I will care for you and the children."

Vorkit nodded thankfully, not daring to raise her eyes, but her heart beat painfully against her ribs.

Lamlam had been angry and jealous, but she had not been able to dissuade her husband and the nights Tariku spent with Vorkit were painful for her. Their friendship suffered and they were barely civil towards one another.

Vorkit bore a son to Tariku, but the baby died within days. Tariku embraced Aklilo's children as his own and he became known as the children's *ingera abat*, adoptive father, and little Izaya from the age of five was already out in the fields helping him to plant a little maize, grains and vegetables. Lamlam, after bearing an only son, became barren and her hatred for Vorkit was common knowledge.

*

The silence in the Hercules army plane was broken only by stifled coughs and the panting of a woman in labour. She lay at the far end of the cramped plane, a *feringh* doctor and nurse attending her. Suddenly there was a lusty cry and some of the strangers called "Mazal tov," their faces wreathed in excited smiles.

Vorkit sat on the floor in the tail end, her children huddled close to her, their large black eyes wide with apprehension. All the adults and children had numbers stuck to their foreheads, so that everyone could be identified.

'Where is Tariku?' she wondered again. They had been together within the confines of the protective ropes, whilst waiting to board the plane. 'Will he leave me now that we are at last on our way to Jerusalem? The children will be without a father... Poor Aklilo, why did you not wait a few years and come together with us all. You would have been alive today.' She sighed. "Izaya," she said, "can you see Tariku?"

The child nodded and whispered in her ear. She turned her cramped body and saw Tariku with Lamlam and her son. He did not turn to look at her and she wondered what her status would be now in their new country.

Refreshments and milk were passed around and the children drank thirstily. The purr of the engines was soothing and Vorkit eased her aching feet out of her tattered shoes. They had had to leave their meagre possessions in Addis Ababa, the few pots and pans and clothing they had carried through the difficult months since they'd left the village to make their way to the city.

When news had come to the elders that the rebel forces were again closing in, that Beta Israel should make their way to Addis Ababa, and that it was imperative to come to the Israeli Embassy to register, they had gathered the villagers together and it was decided to leave as soon as possible. The flocks and the herds were sold at very low prices The *tukuls* were abandoned on land that did not belong to them.

They had walked for weeks, until their feet bled. Part of the way they had been fortunate to ride on bales of straw at the back of a truck. They had gone days without food until the children had cried with hunger. Vorkit had lost touch with Aklilo's family who'd left a few days earlier than she and the children. She supposed that they must be on one of the other planes. 'My parents and my brothers and sisters, she thought excitedly,' sitting upright. 'Perhaps I will see them soon.' Then she remembered the dangers and the horrors they'd experienced so many years ago on the way to Sudan, and her excitement evaporated, leaving an iciness instead. Perhaps they too had been killed, like her beloved Aklilo. Her heart ached for him, and for them.

They had registered together with thousands of their brethren at the Embassy. The rumour had it that they would spend many months in the city, perhaps years before they would be allowed to leave Ethiopia. Tariku had been allotted an allowance for himself, his wife and child, and for Vorkit and the children of Aklilo. The older children had joined the lessons in the makeshift school in the Embassy compound and even Tariku and some of the other young men had joined classes, fearful of being conscripted into Mengistu's army against the rebels.

Vorkit was suddenly aware of the jolt as the plane's wheels were lowered and there was a buzz of excited anticipation. 'It's a dream,' she thought. 'If I pinch myself, I'll wake up in my *tukul* with my children fast asleep beside me.'

The next few hours she remembered in a haze: the hundreds of unfamiliar faces smiling at them, the indistinguishable sounds of a strange language, the blinding light of tens of flashbulbs behind the cameras, the questions, the excitement, the noise. Men and women watched them as they alighted from the bowels of the planes, their eyes moist with tears, unable to hide their emotion at seeing the miraculous arrival of thousands upon thousands of their people.

The first night in the land of Israel was spent at the hotel in Jerusalem, which had been turned into an absorption centre. The new arrivals were dazed with exhaustion. Vorkit shared a room with her two children, whilst Tariku, Lamlam and their son were put into an adjoining room. There was no sign of the rest of the family, who must have been sent to different centres around the country. A few of the village people were at their centre, however, and Vorkit was reassured when she saw familiar faces. She hoped she would be able to locate Aklilo's parents, Mamo, the others, maybe even Uditu, if she'd survived the journey to the Sudanese border.

The long lines began again after breakfast in the large dining hall. The young Ethiopian men and women who'd arrived during Operation Moshe many years before, and who were now fluent in the local language, interpreted for the newcomers.

Vorkit stood in line with Tariku and Lamlam.

"Your names and the names of your children, please..."

"Vorkit Mahari," she answered.

"Ah yes..." the pen was poised in mid-air, whilst the writer stared up at his interpreter. "Zahava Rahamim," translated the young man solemnly.

"Isaya Isaak." She looked lovingly at her eldest child, and he smiled shyly.

"Yeshiyahu Itzchak," said the interpreter. "You must have Hebrew names for registration," he added apologetically. "Also you, Zahava, must take your husband's family name, Itzchak."

Vorkit shrugged. If that is what they wanted, she would oblige but she would always continue to use her father's name, Mahari.

"The little girl is..."

"Konjiet Isaak." Vorkit found it all very baffling. Why would they want them to change their names? They had beautiful names. 'Why, Konjiet means beautiful,' she thought.

"The girl is Yaffa Itzchak," said the interpreter.

It was most confusing for the new immigrants, but they accepted the upheaval stoically, and reverted immediately to their usual names amongst themselves.

Dozens of volunteers had appeared at the hotel, bearing clothes, toys, household goods and food for the immigrants. The latter were told to wait in their rooms until the volunteers came round to fit them with clothing and shoes, and all the other many necessities for daily living. Israeli bystanders came to look bringing their children along with them. Vorkit felt she was on display.

Tariku complained that he was being given orders by women. "Whoever heard of such a thing," he exclaimed indignantly. "These women wear trousers and behave like men, and they do not show the usual respect for the men." He shook his head sadly. "They do not lower their eyes when they speak to me, they instruct me to sit, whilst they measure my feet for shoes, instead of washing my feet as they should with an honoured guest."

When the volunteers had demonstrated the bewildering plumbing arrangements of the toilet and the bath, they had all been perplexed. Who'd have imagined having a bathroom leading off the bedroom! What strange creatures these Jews were and how different from the Beta Israel, and they came from so many different parts of the world. The elders didn't like it at all. In fact they seemed to have lost all their authority. They were like a boat without its rudder.

Days flew by in boredom. The overcrowding was rife and arguments broke out amongst the immigrants. It was many weeks before the authorities were able to register everyone, to fit them out with sets of clothing, household goods, allowances. Beta Israel were anxious to have their own homes, to work and to settle down in their new country as they'd been promised.

On one such morning Vorkit sat with some of her village people in the hotel lobby. Children ran amongst the adults behaving in an unruly manner.

"See how our youngsters have already learned the ways of the country. In the village they did not show such disrespect for their elders," said a woman sadly.

"We must get our own homes, as they promised us," said Vorkit.

"Promises, all promises," said the elder nearest her. "With our people it is better to lose your children, rather than break a promise." He shook his grizzled head, perplexed.

"The food is not fit to eat... we need to make our own *injirra*, our *boneh* and *taleh*," said another.

"They say there is no teff grain in Israel, so how would we make *injirra*?"

"With wheat flour, imagine making *injirra* with wheat flour. How strange it will taste."

The excited chatter at the far end caught their attention. The women ululated in joy. A family had been reunited. There were tears, embraces and much kissing on the cheeks.

"It is the son of the Kess, who left many years ago through Sudan," called one of the women. "He has been searching for weeks for his family, in all the absorption centres."

Vorkit looked longingly in the direction of the excitement. 'If only I could find my parents. If they arrived when they should have, perhaps they too are searching for me.'

Tariku sat down beside her. His eyes were vacant and he perspired heavily. "What is it Tariku?" Vorkit asked softly.

"It is Lamlam, she is weeping. She says she cannot live like this. She wishes for her own *tukul*."

"That is not all that is worrying her," said Vorkit sadly. "You have been fighting about me, is that not so?"

Tariku said nothing but looked at her glumly.

"If I can find my family, it would help. I and the children could live with them."

"Have you asked anyone yet to help find them?"

Vorkit said nothing for a while. How could she explain that she was afraid to ask, in case the news was bad.

"He who knows not how to ask, will not become governor," said Tariku watching her. "You must begin to make enquiries. The young people at the desk in front are there for that purpose. They have been here many years and speak Hebrew fluently but you may talk to them in Amharic. Perhaps they came together with your parents. Come, Vorkit, I will help you."

Vorkit, once she'd made up her mind to search for her parents and for Aklilo's family, began to question everyone. Daily there were family reunions and she always stood aside until she could ask the veterans whether they'd seen the Mahari family, perhaps now called Rahamim, no? Then maybe her in-laws?

No one seemed to have any news of the people she asked for. One of the young men assigned to help in the family reunions had written the information down in a diary and promised to make enquiries. They had been in Jerusalem for three months, when the unbelievable occurred. A handsome, clean-shaven young man stood talking with the Ethiopian veterans who had been assisting in the reunification of families, when Vorkit and Tariku came down to the lobby to sit out another interminable day of boredom.

Vorkit saw one of the men pointing at her and the young man turned and stared, his face wreathed in smiles. Vorkit's heart leapt.

"Tariku," she gasped. "If I didn't know that Aklilo was dead, I would have sworn that it was he: look at the likeness. It is extraordinary."

"Vorkit, it is I, Aklilo, your husband, the father of your children," he said breathlessly.

Neither moved. Vorkit stood frozen to the spot. Tariku ran forward and embraced his friend, but Aklilo's eyes never left her face and he disengaged himself from Tariku's embrace and walked slowly towards his wife. Tears flowed down her cheeks and he put out a hand to brush them away. She kissed his hand and then they kissed excitedly three times on the cheeks.

"How is it that you are alive, when they saw you being shot. Mamo says he saw you being buried," she asked softly.

"I was shot, and was unconscious for some time, then when they buried the others, Uditu noticed that I was still breathing. They put me on the donkey and the Red Cross people came over the border to help us and..."

"Aklilo, I am so happy to see you alive and well," she said hesitantly. "I cannot understand though why, when you arrived in Jerusalem, you did not write or send word that you were alive, or if you could not do so, then why did not Uditu send word?"

Aklilo sighed but remained silent for a long moment. His eyes searched hers, then flickered towards Tariku who hadn't said a word.

"We had news that the village was wiped out by the rebels and that you were all murdered... so there was no one to write to."

"It was the village north of ours..." Tariku spoke for the first time.

"*Ishi*, yes... It was Uditu who saw the village elder Abba Ababe and then we realised the truth. At first neither I nor Uditu could get away, there was so much to do getting our people organised and then, when we were able to do so, Uditu searched in the northern part of the country and I in the centre and the south. But it was she who found my parents, Mamo and the others."

"Where are they Aklilo? I have been searching for them too."

"They are in Eilat, but they wish to join us here, and I am working on it."

"Do you know anything of my family?" Vorkit's voice quavered.

Aklilo hesitated then said quietly, "During the months we spent in the camp on the Sudanese border we were told that they had been shot by the rebels. Only three people from their group survived. I am sorry."

There it was then, the truth she had so feared, but her eyes were dry though she felt numb. "What about my grandparents and uncle and his family?"

"We will search for them, Vorkit, now that I have found you. I would like to see our son and my mother gave me the wonderful news that I have a daughter, Konjiet, and that she is as beautiful as her name."

"They will be here soon, Aklilo, there they are... Isayu, Konjiet, we have found your father, he is not dead as we were told. It is wonderful news, is it not?" She wished she had had time to prepare them and she watched Aklilo limp towards them.

The children stared at Aklilo with wide innocent eyes. "But Tariku is our father," stammered Isayu confused.

Aklilo looked sadly from Tariku to Vorkit and back again. "I had hoped..." he said quietly.

"I will go and bring Lamlam to see you," said Tariku making his getaway.

"It is as you have hoped, my husband," whispered Vorkit. "When it was thought that I was a widow, and that everyone pitied me for not having a man to protect me and the children, it was your good friend Tariku who cared for us. He was very good to the children, and treated them as his own. Do not be angry, Aklilo, it will be hard for him because he has only one child and Lamlam does not make things easy for him."

"It shall be as you say," answered Aklilo.

"What happened to your leg, Aklilo. I noticed that you limp." She watched him questioningly.

"I did not want to tell you so soon..." he said hesitantly, "for fear that when you see that I have no leg you will not want me back."

Vorkit's eyes widened in surprise. "I see you have both legs: what do you mean?"

"When they shot me, they did so in my leg and I lost much blood, that is why they thought I was dead." He watched her.

"*Ishi*," she said.

"The only way they could save my life was to cut off the leg, just above the knee. I walked with crutches which the Red Cross gave me and when I arrived in our country, I was fitted with a wooden leg."

"I do not miss your leg, it is you I love." Vorkit spoke hesitantly. "If you want me, I will be very happy to be your wife once more."

Aklilo's eyes lit up in happiness.

"My husband, I have one question."

"*Ishi*, Vorkit?"

"In all these years, that we have been apart, did you not take another woman?"

Glossary

The following are words and phrases in Hebrew, Yiddish, German, Farsi, Amharic and Arabic. The latter language has many dialects so that a word used in Yemen is often pronounced differently from the same word used in Iraq for example. There is no exact way of spelling these words in English. I have seen so many different versions of the same word but I have tried to be consistent throughout.

A (Arabic) H (Hebrew) Y (Yiddish) G (German) F (Farsi)
Amh (Amharic)

A

abaiyas	Beduin robes
Abba, Abbeh	father
Abu	father
Abu Abdullah	father of Abdullah (A)
aguna	deserted wife who may therefore not get a divorce (H)
Ah sheina meideleh	a pretty young girl
Akel	tax collector
aliyah	(lit.) going up (colloq.) immigrating to Israel (H)
alkhanaka	runaway bride (A)
Allah u Akhbar	God is great (A)
Ashkenazi	Jews of Eastern European descent
Ayatolla	The Head Priest (F)

162

B

baas	boss or master (Afrikaans)
bagrut	matriculation
baradar	brother (F)
berekete	Sabbath bread (Amh)
beriberi	hot spicy meat and lentil sauce (Amh)
Beta Israel	the Ethiopian Jews referred to themselves as such
Bnei Israel	(lit.) sons of Israel, the Indian Jews from the Konkan coast
boneh	coffee ritual (Amh)
Brit Mila	circumcision ceremony

C

| chador | black robe and veil |

D

| darmangah | hospital (F) |
| dhotis | laundrymen (Hindi) |

E

| Eretz | land as in Eretz Israel, the Land of Israel (H) |
| es, es mein liebe kinder | eat, eat my beloved children (Y) |

F

fedayeen	Arab peasants
fedayian	volunteers in acts of suicidal terrorism
feringhi	foreigner
finjan	small long-handled pot for making Turkish coffee (A)

G

| galmuta | woman either divorced or widowed (Amh) |

Gat	green leaf chewed by men of Yemen giving them a feeling of well-being
gazoz	fizzy drink (H)
gharries	carriages

H

hafoekh	(lit.) reversed, used as slang for coffee with milk (H)
hajera	patio (F)
haldi	preparation of turmeric and coconut milk which is rubbed into the skin
halvah	confection made of sesame seeds
haredi	Ultra religious Jew
Hassidim	(lit.) the pious, the Jewish religious sect established in the mid-eighteenth century by the Rabbi Baal Shem Tov
hazan	cantor (H)
Hekhazit	the Front (H)
hilbeh	spice (A)
Histadrut	Israel Trade Union Association (H)
hora	dance of celebration done in a circle where the participants join hands (H)

I

ingera abat	adoptive father (Amh)
injirra	sour spongy pancake like bread (Amh)
Inshallah	God willing or Allah willing (A)
ishi	yes (Amh)

J

jaradock	dried Iraqi pita bread (A)
jebuti	rubber flip-flops with thong between big and second toe
jevena	finjan-like utensil (Amh)
jihad	Moslem war against infidels

joub	canal (F)

K

kamises	kaftan-like robes
kess	priest or Rabbi (Amh)
ketuba	marriage contract
khahar	sister (F)
khamsin	heatwave
khanom	Madam (F)
khorisht	type of spicy stew
khorisht gharmeh sabzi	a spicy vegetable stew
kiddush	ceremonial blessing over wine and bread (H)
koffiya	Arab head-dress or keffiya
kolboynick	plastic basin used for garbage (H)
kolo	roasted chickpeas (Amh)
kumzitz	(lit.) come sit, (colloq.) a barbecue round a bonfire (Y)

L

laccha	hexagonal pendant hanging from necklace of black and gold beads
lakhookh	pancakes made of dura flour (A)

M

maabara (sing.) maabarot (pl.)	tent cities which sprang up in the Fifties in order to absorb the tens of thousands of new immigrants (H)
makolet	small grocery shop (H)
Malida	thanksgiving ceremony with platter of five fruits, cardamom spice, rose water, rice cakes, nuts and raisins
Mashiah	Messiah
Mazal Tov	good luck or congratulations (H)
meher	rains before the sowing of the harvest (Amh)

mehndi	henna ceremony for the bride (Marathi)
meideleh	little girl, usually used endearingly
meine tirer neshoomer	my dear soul (Y)
Mekorot	the government water company (H)
mezzuzah	a Judaic scroll attached to the doorpost (H)
mil'uim	army reserve duty (H)
Mohel	someone trained to do circumcisions (H)
Mujahedin	Islamic volunteeers in acts of terrorism (F)
Mukhtar	chief of village
Mukkadam	head of secular community (Marathi)
mullahs	Iranian priests (F)

N

Nag panchami	Hindi festival taking place on the fifth day of the fifth Hindi month, Shravan (August) when women take part in the cobra ceremony
nargillah	water pipe (A)

P

Palamidas	Skipjack tuna fish
Pesach	Passover festival (H)
pishkesh	a tip or baksheesh (F)
puris	Indian deep fried dumplings

R

Ramadan	Moslem festival lasting a month where the people fast during the day and eat only after sundown
Raus	out (German)
Rehov	street (H)
Rosh Hashanna	Jewish New Year (H)

S

sambousak	crescent shaped pastry filled with spiced meat or goats' cheese or almonds
samneh	clarified butter (A)
Savta	grandmother (H)
seder	the festive ceremony and dinner on the first evening of Passover (H)
Shabbat	Sabbath (H)
shalom	meaning peace and used as a greeting (H) sholom (Y)
sharav	heatwave (H)
sheitel	wig (Y)
shiddach	matchmaking or an arranged marriage
shikun	small government-owned flat (H)
shiva	the ritual Jewish mourning period
shreit	scream (Y)
Shurah	armed self defence of the Iraqi Zionist underground
sindur powder	(pronounced sindoor) red lead powder
Siyit	Madam (A)
skhoog	hot chilli tomato paste (A)
Solel Boneh	government owned building contracting firm (H)

T

taleh	yellow beer-like drink (Amh)
Tnuva	one of the main dairy producers in the country
tukul	hut (Amh)

U

ulpan	school for learning Hebrew invariably for new immigrants (H)
Uma, Imma	mother

Y

Yahoudi	Jew (A)
Yishuv	Jewish settlement in Palestine before the state of Israel was proclaimed
Yom Haatzmaut	Day of Independence (H)
Yom Kippur	Day of Atonement and Fasting (H)